# GREEK MYTHOLOGY FOR KIDS

EXPLORE TIMELESS TALES & BEDTIME STORIES FROM ANCIENT GREECE. MYTHS, HISTORY, FANTASY & ADVENTURES OF THE GODS, GODDESSES, TITANS, HEROES, MONSTERS & MORE

HISTORY BROUGHT ALIVE

# FREE BONUS FROM HBA: EBOOK BUNDLE

Greetings!

First of all, thank you for reading our books. As fellow passionate readers of History and Mythology, we aim to create the very best books for our readers.

Now, we invite you to join our VIP list. As a welcome gift, we offer the History & Mythology Ebook Bundle below for free. Plus you can be the first to receive new books and exclusives! Remember it's 100% free to join.

Simply scan the QR code to join.

THE
VIKINGS
FREE
DOWNLOAD

# CONTENTS

**GREEK MYTHOLOGY FOR KIDS: EXPLORE TIMELESS TALES & BEDTIME STORIES FROM ANCIENT GREECE. MYTHS, HISTORY, FANTASY & ADVENTURES OF THE GODS, GODDESSES, TITANS, HEROES, MONSTERS & MORE**

# INTRODUCTION

If you have heard about the Olympic Games, you have heard of the Greeks. Want to know the connection? Here it is.

The first Olympic Games ever was held in a place called Olympia in Greece about 3,000-odd years ago. The people who lived there were called Greeks. Greece is still there—a country of great beauty that you can visit—and the people are still called Greeks.

The myths or stories we are about to talk about were all thought up by very clever men who lived in Greece 2,500 years ago. Greece was famous for its intelligent and thoughtful people. These stories are about how the Earth came into being and about gods, goddesses, heroes, and monsters—some very brave heroes and some very nasty monsters.

The Greek gods and goddesses were almost like us humans. They got angry, they were jealous, and they behaved like ordinary people. But they were gods, so they had extraordinary superpowers, somewhat like Superman!

Why do we need to read and understand these stories? They were written thousands of years ago. The reason is that these stories are great tales! They are full of adventure and excitement. They are fun to read, as you will soon discover. And from these stories, you will learn about how people who made up these stories thought about the world around them.

You will be introduced to Poseidon, the god of the Oceans, who lives deep down in the ocean somewhere. The next time you are out on the sea, look down into the water and see if you can spot him! He might actually be there—you never know! That's the beauty of myths. They keep your mind alive with interesting thoughts.

Now, why do you think they imagined a god who ruled the oceans? Well, let's see—years ago the Greeks did not have giant ships going across oceans regularly. They also did not have the scientific equipment to look into the ocean depths. So, the vast oceans were scary, especially when great storms raged across them. The Greeks were convinced that there was a god who caused the storms when angry. They gave this god a name—Poseidon.

So did many other ancient cultures. They too had gods for the oceans, the heavens, and the winds. Even for thunder and lightning! Now ask yourself this: How did all these people think alike? Remember, 2,500 years ago there were no phones, computers, TV—nothing. There were no airplanes either. So, people from one culture could not just pass on their ideas of gods and goddesses to others around the world. Strange, isn't it?

All important cultures had their own myths. There are the Nordic myths, Egyptian myths, Chinese myths, Indian myths, and many more. Myths were very important to people in ancient times. All these myths are also stories about powerful gods, bold heroes, and eventually, ferocious monsters. Only their names are different.

Why were myths necessary? When lightning was seen, it was frightening to say the least. No one knew why it looked like a bolt from the heavens, and the rumbling thunder that came with it made the thing scarier. To explain this, they made up a god of lightning and thunder. When he was angry, this god would cause the lightning and that awful thunder. It gave people a kind of comfort. The gods were doing it. If they prayed to the gods, they would be safe. Today we know what causes thunderstorms, but back then, no one knew.

You may think that ancient cultures needed heroes like Hercules, for example (we shall be meeting him in this book). But think again! You have modern-day heroes: Superman, Spiderman, and Batman, among many others. We need heroes too! And there is another very interesting thing to notice. The words "Herculean Task" are still used and mean a job that is very difficult and needs superhuman abilities to do. So you see, the ancient myths are still around and alive even thousands of years later! Their names are still used!

The terrific thing about myths is that they make your mind soar as you begin to think of the daring acts that the gods performed. You begin to wonder and become curious. Did they really do those things? All great scientists also had this quality of wonder and curiosity. That is what made them discover and invent all the wonderful things that we see and use today.

Did you ever think that it would be nice to have someone like Spiderman around? He could save lives and rescue people from all sorts of dangers. Most people want this in their hearts. But he isn't real, is he? He is a modern myth, just like Hercules of the Greeks! So hero myths are still being created. They haven't gone away. The only difference is in their names. Think about it. The popularity of these imaginary characters means that we still need myths—heroic myths most of all.

The Greek myths are full of action and adventure. The gods too fight wars and call upon monsters to help them in battle.

We will begin with the creation of the Earth and the heavens, as the myths call it. We can also call it the sky. Without the Earth and the sky, the gods have nothing to rule over. They also need people—mankind. There is a myth about how the first humans were created and how they learned to grow food and use fire.

There are many characters in the Greek myths, and we shall be dealing with all the important ones—the gods who were major players in the Greek imagination.

You must understand that different gods became important at different times. Some were deprived of their power and imprisoned and some were just cast out. But how all these things happened forms the basis of these myths and stories.

The story of the creation of the Earth is common to mythologies everywhere in the world. There are differences of course, but every myth talks of gods and goddesses creating the Earth and bringing mankind to live on it. Without mankind, the gods really would have nothing, and you would not have any myths to read. The Greek gods needed mankind to talk about them and write about them. They made mankind and everything else, after all.

However, there is something that you should know: The Greeks actually believed in their gods and prayed to them, offering them food to keep them happy. They thought that their gods were there from the beginning of time and were the ones who created everything. Today, science calls the origin of the universe the "Big Bang." The interesting part is that the Big Bang happened from a void in space—a black hole! It seems that the Greeks had the correct idea about the creation of the cosmos. Of course, they did not know about black holes, they could only guess.

Now we move on to the Greek myths. Who were the Titans? What did they do? Who were the great heroes? In Greek mythology, there are many heroes, and they are very brave and adventurous people. They undertook almost impossible tasks, and they usually succeeded in doing them. Then there are the gods and goddesses—the Divine men and women who ruled the skies, the oceans, the animals, and the lives of the first humans on Earth.

# CHAPTER 1: HOW THE WORLD WAS CREATED

In the beginning, a long, long time ago…

There was darkness and a void. Nothing else. The universe had not yet been created. The Greeks gave a name to this darkness: Chaos. This was a time before anything existed.

Then Gaia appeared from the void. She was the mother goddess, the universe in divine form.

However, Gaia felt lonely, as she was alone in the universe. So, she created Uranus—the night sky—and made him so big that he covered everything. You do see the sky wherever you look, right? Then she created the mountains and the seas. But she was still alone, except for Uranus of course.

Gaia fell in love with Uranus and married him. They had 12 children. Six of these were female and their names were: Theia, Themis, Mnemosyne, Phoebe, Tethys, and Rhea. The names of the six male children were: Oceanus, Coeus, Crius, Hyperion, Iapetus, and Cronus.

They were called the Titans. Of the six male children, the youngest one, Cronus, is important, and we shall soon see why. These children were the first race on Earth and they were gods too.

As time went by, Gaia realized that Uranus was a cruel person who treated their children badly. Gaia wanted to be rid of him and asked her sons and daughters to help. She went to 11 of them, but they all refused to help her. They were all scared of Uranus. Then she went to the youngest, Cronus. He agreed to help his mother and destroyed Uranus. But before dying, Uranus cursed Cronus, saying that "one day your son will take power away from you in the same way that you took it from me."

Cronus then took the place of Uranus and became the new ruler. Cronus, however, was not a nice ruler. He remembered the curse that Uranus had put on him and began swallowing all the children his wife Rhea gave birth to. He thought that it was the best way to stop the curse from taking effect. He swallowed five of his children before Rhea decided to stop him from swallowing the next baby, which she knew was a boy.

Rhea went to Gaia and asked for help in saving her sixth child. Gaia told her what to do. When the sixth baby was born, Rhea secretly took him and left him in a cave on the island of Crete. There, the baby was looked after by Nymphs (goddesses of nature) and he grew up big and strong. To fool Cronus, Rhea wrapped a piece of rock in cloth and gave it to him. Cronus, believing it to be his sixth baby, swallowed it!

Rhea named the baby Zeus, and when he was old enough, the Nymphs told him how his father had swallowed his five brothers and sisters. This made Zeus angry and he decided that he would find his father and defeat him in battle.

Zeus then summoned Metis, daughter of Oceanus to his aid. Metis was known for her wisdom. She gave Zeus a potion with instructions to give it to Cronus. Zeus quietly introduced the potion into Cronus's drink. As soon as Cronus drank it he vomited, and out came all the babies he had swallowed, fully grown and alive. Zeus gathered his brothers and sisters—Hera, Poseidon, Hades, Hestia, and Demeter—and declared war on his father Cronus.

The battle continued for close to 10 years with no real result. Neither side could defeat the other. It was at this time that Mother Earth, Gaia, came to Zeus and revealed to him that he should seek the help of the three Cyclops and the three Hecatoncheires—monsters she had also given birth to. She told him that Uranus, their father, seeing how ugly they were, banished them and kept them locked up. Mother Earth advised Zeus to release them. Zeus went to the monsters and realized that they also hated Cronus. He had continued to keep them locked up after seizing power from Uranus, so they agreed to fight for Zeus. These were terrible creatures with superhuman powers! The Cyclops were giants with magical powers that had one eye in the middle of their foreheads. They made weapons that could hurl thunder and lightning at the enemy, and they gave these weapons to Zeus. The Hecatoncheires were also giants with 100 arms and 50 heads and could not be killed easily. The battle was about to become very nasty.

Zeus went to war with Cronus with his new army and the weapons are given to him by the Cyclops. The monsters too went with him, and in no time, he defeated Cronus. Zeus then sent Cronus and the Titans to an underground place called the Underworld, or the Land Of The Dead. There they were guarded by the Hecatoncheires so that they could never escape. Zeus was now the new ruler!

## THE TITAN CHILDREN

Some of the Titan children who were not imprisoned by Zeus played very important roles in the affairs of humans.

Cronus, his wife Rhea, and Zeus are well-known in Greek mythology. However, the sons of Iapetus (who was Cronus's brother)—Prometheus, Atlas, and Epimetheus—are also important gods, about whom we shall now read.

### THE ORIGIN OF MANKIND

Prometheus and Epimetheus were brothers. When the war was going on between Zeus and the Titans, Prometheus warned the Titans that Zeus had the Cyclops and the Hecatoncheires on his side and that the Titans should change their battle plans. The Titans did not listen, so Prometheus and Epimetheus went over to the side of Zeus. When Zeus won the war, he decided to reward Prometheus and Epimetheus for supporting him. This decision, as you will see, was very important for many reasons.

Zeus called Prometheus and asked him to create mankind. Prometheus took clay and water and fashioned humans. A goddess named Athena breathed life into the clay models and they came alive. These were the first humans.

Epimetheus was given the task of making the animals, birds, and insects. He worked carefully and gave each creature a means of protection. He gave the turtle a hard shell, the bee a sting, and the snake its venom. Prometheus, meanwhile, was busy making humans. He was slow and when he was finally done, he realized that Epimetheus had used up all the protective devices by giving them away to the animals, birds, and insects. There was nothing left to give mankind. Prometheus scratched his head. Mankind needed some form of protection. He thought of fire. The gods had a fire, so if he wanted to give it to the humans, he would need to ask permission from the ruler, Zeus.

Prometheus went to Zeus and asked him, "O great ruler, the humans need fire to protect themselves and to prepare food. With your permission, I will give them fire." But Zeus flatly refused, saying that only the gods had the right to have the fire. This enraged Prometheus. He had never forgiven Zeus for destroying the Titans since he was a Titan himself. Prometheus was determined to give fire to the humans. "I don't need your consent Zeus—I will give the humans fire." He went to the island of Lemnos and stole fire from the forges of Hephaestus (another god). He carried it to mankind and gave it to them. Fire, as we all know, is very important. Without it food cannot be cooked, and candles cannot be lit!

When Prometheus arrived with the fire the people were scared of this glowing light. Prometheus then taught them what to do with it. He showed them how to cook meat, melt iron to make weapons, and how to use fire to scare away wild animals. The people slowly understood the importance of this element called fire and began to worship it.

Prometheus liked the humans more than the gods. But for his theft of fire, Zeus would make him pay a heavy price.

At night, Zeus, on his usual journey through the heavens, saw several lights on Earth and realized that they were small fires. How did they get fire? Then he knew. That fellow Prometheus must have given it to them. The next morning he summoned Hephaestus, the master metal workman. "Prepare chains of such strength that no one can break them. They must be made so that they last for eternity!" barked Zeus.

Hephaestus asked, "and what are these chains to be used for?"

Zeus told him. Hephaestus was aghast. But he went away to make the chains. He did not dare annoy Zeus.

Zeus had Prometheus bound by chains to a rock and had a very large eagle come and feast on his liver. During the day the bird would eat his liver, and during the night it would grow back again. The next day the bird would be back to eat the now grown liver. Zeus wanted Prometheus to feel the pain every day. But Prometheus never surrendered to Zeus.

This carried on for about 30,000 years! Until, with the permission of Zeus, Hercules (a popular Greek hero) unchained Prometheus, and killed the dreadful flying creature that was feasting on his liver.

Now you will read about another Greek god, whose name you are probably familiar with—Atlas. Atlas was a Titan, and he had commanded the Titan army. After the defeat of the Titans, Zeus had a special punishment for him. He sent Atlas to the end of Earth and had him hold up the sky for all eternity so that the sky and the Earth shall never meet. They are still separate today. A collection of maps in book form is called an Atlas, in his honor, even today. You see, mythical figures and their impact are still here among us!

Zeus set up his palace on Mount Olympus and went to live there. He decided that the universe was too big for one man to rule, so he needed to have a lottery. The important Olympian gods and goddesses would all draw straws to see who got what to rule over. There were twelve of them. Let's see who they were.

Among the gods there was Zeus, then Poseidon, Hephaestus, Hermes, Ares, and Apollo. Among the goddesses, there was Hera, Athena, Artemis, Hestia, Aphrodite, and finally Demeter. You will get to know who they all were soon.

Zeus was the most powerful, so he got rulership over Ether, which meant that he had lordship over the heavens.

Poseidon was given control over the oceans and Hades was given power over the Underworld. These were the main gods.

The goddesses got positions too. Hesta got to rule over hearth and home, Hera was given marriage and childbirth, and Demeter was made goddess of the harvest. It is important to understand that the rulership of the gods and goddesses was over the affairs of humans, on Earth.

Ares was made a god of war and Hermes was the messenger. Hephaestus was made a god of fire and Apollo became the god of light and music.

Artemis became the goddess of hunting and Athena ruled over wisdom. Aphrodite was given power over love.

One day, Dionysus turned up at Mount Olympia. Since he never came to the Council, he had no place to sit. All the thrones were occupied. Hesta, who was Zeus's eldest sister, gave up her place to Dionysus. She wanted to go and look after the fire in the palace—a fire that always burned. Dionysus had power over nature, wine, and fruitfulness, so he was an important god, especially for the humans, who needed their trees to produce fruit.

Now, we come to the stories that tell of wonderful adventures by the gods and goddesses, and of course, the heroes.

# CHAPTER 2: THE LABORS OF HERCULES (PART 1)

The first hero you will read about is Hercules. He had to complete the 12 labors given to him. Each one was a very difficult task, but first, you have to know why Hercules was given those difficult and dangerous tasks.

Let us start at the birth of Hercules to understand the reason.

Perseus was the son of Zeus and Danae. Zeus had announced publicly that the first male descendant of Perseus would rule after him. Hera, the wife of Zeus, did not want the son of Perseus to become ruler. So she played a trick and got Eurystheus installed as ruler.

Eurystheus was the grandson of Perseus. Hercules, who was born soon after, never became king. Hera continued to trouble Hercules through Eurystheus, and the most troublesome and difficult jobs were given to Hercules. But he was equal to the tasks.

Hercules showed his strength when he was an infant. Two fearful serpents entered his room. They attacked Hercules, but he was strong. He grabbed one serpent in each hand and wrung their necks. The serpents were sent by Hera to kill Hercules.

When Hercules grew up, he made a mistake and harmed his own family. This too was the doing of Hera, who had sent a disease that made Hercules lose his mind.

Eurystheus, on the advice of the Delphic Oracle, punished Hercules by giving him 12 tasks so that he could be pardoned for his sin. The story of each of these tasks is an adventure by itself. Let us see what Hercules had to do and how he finally succeeded in completing all the tasks successfully.

## THE NEMEAN LION (THE FIRST LABOR OF HERCULES)

King Eurystheus, who did not like Hercules much, decided to give Hercules a dangerous task as his first. Hercules arrived at the court and stood expectantly, waiting for Eurystheus to tell him what his first task was.

Eurystheus thought for a moment. "You will go to Nemea and kill the Nemean lion."

"Should I bring the dead lion back here?" Hercules asked.

Eurystheus was annoyed. "What am I going to do with a dead lion? Besides, by the time you bring it here, it will stink. Just bring back its hide. That will do."

Hercules nodded and left the court.

Hercules was aware that so far nobody could kill this lion and that it was terrorizing a place called Nemea. Hercules set out to kill the lion, not knowing if he could really do it.

Arriving at a town called Cleonae, Hercules rested for the night at the house of a poor man called Molorchus. When Molorchus heard that Hercules had come to kill the terrible lion, he was afraid. He wanted to offer a sacrifice. Hercules asked him to wait for 30 days. If he came back victorious, they would perform a sacrifice to honor Zeus.

Hercules then set out to where the lion lived. He knew that this was no ordinary lion, but an extremely strong and fierce animal that no one till now had been able to kill. Hercules began tracking the lion. And suddenly he saw it! He took out his bow and arrows and began shooting at the lion. But although the arrows found their mark, nothing happened to the lion. Hercules now knew that there was only one option left. He picked up his club and approached the lion. The lion disappeared into a cave that Hercules saw had two entrances. He quickly went and blocked one of the entrances. He then entered the cave through the other.

Hercules grabbed the lion and put his strong arms around his neck and held on hard. As you can imagine, there was a terrible battle. The lion was strong and wanted to throw Hercules off. But slowly the lion began to lose strength and finally died. Hercules then took the hide of the lion and went back to Cleonae, to the poor man's house. There he offered a sacrifice to Zeus.

Triumphant Hercules returned to Eurystheus in Mycenae. He had made a cloak out of the skin of the lion and was wearing it when he appeared before Eurystheus. The cloak made him invincible! The king was frightened when he saw Hercules wearing the lion's skin, complete with its head. He did look like a wild and dangerous man.

He decided to send messages to Hercules, instead of calling him to the court.

## THE LERNEAN HYDRA (THE SECOND LABOR OF HERCULES)

Eurystheus wanted Hercules to fail, so he began to think until he had an idea. He immediately wrote out a message, "kill the Lernean Hydra," and sent it by messenger to Hercules. Eurystheus chuckled to himself. The serpent would certainly kill Hercules. Eurystheus knew how dangerous the Hydra was.

The Lernean Hydra was a terrifying serpent with nine heads! It was huge and lived in the swamps of a place called Lernaea. Another thing about this serpent? One of its heads was immortal! That also meant that as soon as any one of the nine heads was cut off, two heads would grow back again. So you could really not kill it. That was the problem that Hercules faced. It was also said that the breath of the serpent was so vile that it killed whoever stood in front of it.

This time Hercules took his nephew Iolaus with him. Iolaus was an expert charioteer, so Hercules and Iolaus went in search of the serpent on a chariot. They drove to Lernaea and arrived at the swamp where the serpent had its lair. But it was hiding deep in the swamp and Hercules knew that entering the swamp to fight the Hydra was a bad idea. The serpent would be in its element! Hercules decided to draw him out of the swamp to better tackle him.

Hercules fired flaming arrows into the swamp, and the Hydra came out of the murky waters to see who would dare disturb its lair. Hercules, seeing the terrifying creature, knew that he was in for a tough battle. He used his sword to cut off the heads, but as soon as he cut off one of the heads, two heads grew back again! Hercules realized that he was getting nowhere. The Hydra also had a friend—a giant crab—who came out of the swamp and began attacking Hercules. It kept on biting Hercules on his foot.

*Better get rid of this nuisance first*, thought Hercules, and he killed the crab with one blow of his club. Then he asked Iolaus to light a fire and use a piece of wood fashioned as a burning torch.

Hercules then told Iolaus to burn the headless stump of the neck after he had cut off the head so that the nerve endings would be destroyed. This Iolaus did, and the heads did not grow back again.

Finally, after a grim battle, Hercules cut off the last head, which was immortal. Taking it, he quickly buried it in a hole and placed a huge rock on top. The Hydra could not get at the head and die. Hercules then cut open the serpent and dipped his arrows in the serpent's blood. It was said to be extremely poisonous.

Hercules appeared at the court of Eurystheus and reported the killing of the Lernean Hydra. This enraged Eurystheus even more.

## THE HIND OF CERYNEIA (THE THIRD LABOR OF HERCULES)

This time Eurystheus decided to give Hercules a task that he was sure would be impossible for him to perform. Hercules would have to bring back a specific hind that lived in Ceryneia. First of all, let's see what a 'hind' is. It is in fact, just a female deer.

It sounds like an easy job for someone as powerful as Hercules, right? Well, partly right. There is a catch. This particular deer had golden horns and bronze hooves, and it was a pet of Artemis, the goddess of hunting. Killing an animal that was a pet of a goddess was not easy, so Hercules was in a dilemma. He decided to chase the deer. The deer kept getting away but Hercules kept after it. After almost a year passed by, the deer was finally exhausted. It went to a mountain to rest. As she was crossing a stream, Hercules shot her with an arrow. He picked up the carcass and started on his way back to Mycenae to show Eurystheus. But on the way, Artemis and Apollo appeared and Artemis was extremely angry seeing her pet deer dead. Hercules then told Artemis of the tasks he had to perform in order to be pardoned for his sin. Artemis forgave Hercules, and with her powers, brought the deer back to life. But she made Hercules promise to bring the deer back alive once his task was complete. Hercules agreed. Happy at this turn of events, he took the live deer to the court of Eurystheus.

Eurystheus liked the deer and decided to keep it. Hercules then said, "O great king, Artemis, and Apollo made me promise to take the deer back alive. If you keep it, I will have made a false promise and be punished. But Artemis and Apollo will also punish you."

Eurystheus did not want Artemis and Apollo after him. He released the deer.

## THE WILD ERYMANTHIAN BOAR (THE FOURTH LABOR OF HERCULES)

Before we get to the story of how Hercules accomplished his task, let's talk about wild boars. These are fearsome animals—big, strong, and with tusks. They are irritable and attack if disturbed, and bigger animals steer clear of them.

The task set for Hercules this time was to bring the wild Erymanthian boar back alive. Can you imagine bringing a big wild boar back alive? But that was what Hercules had to accomplish.

Eurystheus told his courtiers that this time Hercules would not come back. "The boar is bound to kill him. No one has ever come back alive," he said, rubbing his hands in glee.

Hercules, when he received the message from Eurystheus, went to the court of Eurystheus and asked, "you want the boar brought here? Alive?"

Eurystheus was beside himself with joy. "Yes, alive. I sent you the message. Can't you read?"

Hercules did not say a word and quietly left the court. He understood that Eurystheus wanted him to fail.

Hercules knew that this boar came charging down from the mountain called Erymanthus, and destroyed everything in its path, killing whoever got in its way. Its tusks were dangerous weapons and gored humans and animals alike. Everyone was afraid of the boar.

Hercules did not have trouble finding the animal. He could hear it crashing around and destroying things. Hercules chased the boar round and round the mountain, shouting as loudly as he could so as to scare the animal. Finally, the boar, now tired and scared, hid inside a bush. Hercules thought quickly and thrust his spear into the bush and drove the boar out into an area that had thick snow. Once there, the boar could not run and Hercules threw a net and captured him. He took the animal alive to Eurystheus. Seeing Hercules with the huge boar, alive, scared the living daylights out of Eurystheus. He quickly sent Hercules on his way and released the boar. Who would want to keep a large boar around?

## CLEANING THE AUGEAN STABLES (THE FIFTH LABOR OF HERCULES)

Eurystheus now hated Hercules even more. Whatever he gave Hercules to do, he did it. So he thought up a real dirty task that would be impossible to do. Or so he thought.

The task was to clean up the stables of King Augeas. This king was very rich and had thousands of heads of cattle. They were all kept in large stables. There were so many cows, bulls, sheep, goats, and horses that no one had cleaned the stables for years. (You can imagine the smell and the muck that had accumulated over the years!) Eurystheus added one important rule—the cleaning up would have to be finished in a day!

*Now, my friend, we shall see if you can pull off this one!* Eurystheus thought to himself.

Hercules immediately realized that this was going to be a task where he would certainly get dirty, and smelly! But he was determined to do it.

When Hercules arrived at the palace of King Augeas, he saw the stables and all the fine cattle that the king possessed. He wanted some of the cattle from King Augeas, so he devised a plan. He approached the king and said that he would clean the stables in one day if the king promised him a portion of his cattle. The king was so astonished to hear Hercules say that he would clean a large number of stables in a day, that he agreed. Hercules now brought the son of the king to watch. He wanted a witness.

Hercules went to the cattle yard where all the stables were located and broke down a part of the wall on one side, making an opening. He then went to the opposite side and made another similar opening.

Next, he dug large trenches leading from the cattle yard to the two rivers that flowed nearby. Once the trenches reached the river, the water began rushing through them, straight into the yard through one of the wall openings and out the other. The rushing waters carried all the filth and muck with them as they raced through the yard.

Miracle of miracles! All the stables were absolutely clean within no time. Hercules had kept his word. But the king, when he heard that Eurystheus was behind this task, refused to honor his word and give the promised cattle to Hercules. He asked Hercules to leave the kingdom and never return. But Hercules had still completed his task.

## THE STYMPHALIAN BIRDS (THE SIXTH LABOR OF HERCULES)

By this time, Eurystheus was not sure what task to give Hercules. Then he suddenly had an idea. He sent a message to Hercules saying that he must drive away from the enormous flock of vicious birds that gathered at a lake near the town of Stymphalus. This was a very large flock of birds, and they were not ordinary birds, but ferocious ones, as they ate human flesh. Hercules could not decide how to shoo away such a large concentration of birds. But at this point, the goddess Athena came to his rescue. She gave him a clapper, which made a very loud sound and told him to use it to drive the birds away. These iron clappers were made by the master craftsman called Hephaestus, and made a very loud sound. Hercules went up a mountain and from the top, using the clappers. The clappers made such a racket that the startled birds all took to flight. Hercules started firing his arrows at them as they started flying. This time too, with a little help from a goddess, Hercules had succeeded. The myth does not say whether Hercules killed all the birds or only some of them.

But he certainly succeeded in driving them all away. The task was complete.

*Now let's see what that rogue Eurystheus has in mind*, thought Hercules as he made his way back to Mycenae.

# CHAPTER 3: THE LABORS OF HERCULES (PART 2)

## THE CRETAN BULL (THE SEVENTH LABOR OF HERCULES)

For the seventh task, Eurystheus wanted Hercules to go and subdue a fierce bull that was terrorizing the kingdom of King Minos and bring it back to him.

King Minos had created this monster by breaking a promise he made to Poseidon. The sea god had given Minos a big bull with the understanding that Minos would sacrifice it in his honor. But Minos liked the bull and sacrificed another bull. Poseidon, when he got to know of this treachery, turned the bull into a fierce animal that began terrorizing Crete, where Minos lived. Minos did not know what to do. He called upon the only man he knew who could do something. He called Hercules, and Hercules was already on his way to Crete to complete his seventh task.

When he got to Crete, he quite easily controlled the beast. He grabbed the bull's horns and wrestled it to the ground using his enormous strength and took the bull back to Eurystheus.

Terrified at the sight of the bull, Eurystheus screamed. "Take it away! Take it outside!"

Hercules took the bull outside and tethered it. He waited for Eurystheus to say what was to be done.

Eurystheus did a strange thing. He let the bull go free and it began its terrorizing activities again. As to why Eurystheus did what he did, we are not sure. Ultimately, another Greek hero, Theseus, killed the Cretan bull. There were lots of heroes in Greek myths, as you will soon see.

## THE HORSES OF DIOMEDES (THE EIGHTH LABOR OF HERCULES)

The myth or story of this task is not very clear. Eurystheus asked Hercules to go and tame the wild man-eating horses of a ruler named Diomedes and bring them back to Mycenae.

Hercules set off on his journey to Bistone where Diomedes lived and where the horses roamed freely. Hercules knew that the Bistones would fight him if he tried to take the horses away, but he was ready for the fight. He attacked the Bistones and defeated and killed them. He then went to the palace and killed Diomedes too.

Hercules tamed the horses and took them back to Eurystheus. But to everyone's surprise, Eurystheus let them go free! Hercules, however, had completed his eighth task, and he was not worried by this strange behavior of the king.

## HIPPOLYTE'S BELT (THE NINTH LABOR OF HERCULES)

The ninth labor of Hercules is very interesting. It involves a tribe of women warriors who were called the Amazons. They lived separately from everyone else and were great fighters. Their queen, Hippolyte, wore special armor in the form of a belt given to her by Ares, the Greek god of war, as she was the bravest warrior.

Eurystheus knew about this special belt and wanted it for his daughter. He cleverly sent Hercules to bring him the belt.

"Don't worry my dear, if anyone can bring back the belt, Hercules can," he told his daughter.

Hercules knew that the Amazons would not easily give up the queen or her belt. He decided to take men with him to help, in case there was a battle of some kind.

Some say the belt that Hippolyte wore was made of gold and it offered her divine protection in times of battle. That's why Eurystheus was interested in it.

Hercules gathered some of his friends, including the brave warrior Theseus, and set sail for the land of the Amazons. When they arrived at the harbor, Hercules was not sure what to do. Then he saw that the queen herself had come to visit him. Hercules greeted the queen. "Why have you come?" was the first question that Hippolyte asked of him. She probably knew why Hercules had come. Hercules, without hesitation, told her that he had come to take her belt and carry it back to Mycenae.

The queen seemed to be ready to hand over the belt to Hercules without a fight. But here, another goddess, Hera, arrived to play tricks. Hera knew that Hippolyte would give Hercules the belt and was determined to stop that from happening.

Hera disguised herself as an Amazon warrior and went around telling all the other warriors that Hercules had come to fight a war and kidnap their queen. Since Hera was a woman like themselves and was dressed as a warrior, they believed her.

The Amazon warriors decided to attack Hercules before he could attack them. They had to protect their queen. Unaware of what was going on, Hercules waited on his ship for Hippolyte to come to give him the belt as she had promised. The only one who grew suspicious was Theseus. "They are going to attack us. I can feel it in my bones," he told Hercules. Hercules was still not sure that the Amazons were preparing to attack them. Hercules, of course, did not believe Theseus. But a little later, he saw the Amazon warriors all dressed up in armor coming towards their ship. They were armed. Hercules realized that they were going to be attacked and drew his sword. So did the other men in the ship.

A massive battle ensued. Hercules was forced to kill Hippolyte, as she was leading the battle. She too had been fooled by Hera into thinking that Hercules wanted to kidnap her and take her away. Hercules removed the belt and sailed away. He later presented the belt to Eurystheus, thus completing the ninth labor.

## THE CATTLE OF GERYON (THE TENTH LABOR OF HERCULES)

Hercules now waited for the tenth labor. He was sure that Eurystheus would think up something very difficult and dangerous. Sure enough, he received a message from Eurystheus that he was to deliver his cattle from the monster Geryon.

Geryon was no ordinary monster. Chrysaor and Callirhoe were his parents. Chrysaor had appeared from Gorgon Medusa's body (whom we shall read about later). This meant that Geryon was an exceptionally strong and dangerous character. He had three legs and heads—all in one body! That really made him look odd, but that's the way he was. You might be wondering how he got around with six legs, but it seems that he managed quite well.

Hercules realized that to finish this task, he would have to travel to the island of Erythia. Geryon lived on that island and he kept a herd of cattle that were red in color. The cattle were guarded by Orthos, a hound with two heads, and by a herdsman called Eurytion.

The sun, in his admiration, gave Hercules a golden goblet to sail in. It was a large goblet, that much is sure because Hercules was no small man. He set sail for the island where the cattle were.

As soon as he arrived at the island, the two-headed dog attacked Hercules. But it was no match for his strength. One blow from his mighty club killed the two-headed dog. The herdsman, seeing the death of the dog, came to stop Hercules, but was met with the same fate. Hercules was in no mood to play around. He had a job to do. But another herdsman who had seen what had just happened went to Geryon and told him about Hercules. Geryon, being a monster, was enraged and came out to fight Hercules. But he had no chance. Hercules killed him with his arrows.

However, Hercules now faced a bigger problem. How could he drive a whole herd of cattle from Erythia to Mycenae? The island was far away from Mycenae, and to travel with a herd of cattle was beginning to look extremely difficult.

Hercules knew that he had to find a way and started on his journey. In a place called Liguria, the sons of the god Poseidon tried to steal the cattle from him. Hercules killed them. But this, as he saw later, was the least of his problems.

When he was traveling through a place called Rhegium, one of the bulls escaped, jumped into the sea, and swam to a neighboring country (this country is now called Italy). The ruler, Eryx, who was another one of Poseidon's sons, found the bull and put it in his own herd. Hercules, meanwhile, was trying to find the bull and finally tracked it to Eryx's kingdom. He asked Eryx to return the animal, but Eryx refused, saying that he would give the bull back only if Hercules could beat him at arm wrestling. Feats of strength were what Hercules loved. He agreed and not only defeated Eryx but killed him. He took back the bull and put it back in his herd.

After a long and tedious journey, Hercules was close to Mycenae. He thought he had made it, but did not reckon with the evil Hera who wanted to create problems for him. Hera sent a gadfly to disturb and irritate the cattle. The herd scattered in different directions to escape the flying insect. Hercules spent time running around and brought the herd together again. Finally, he delivered them to Eurystheus.

## THE APPLES OF THE HESPERIDES (THE ELEVENTH LABOR OF HERCULES)

After the tiring tenth labor, Hercules was exhausted. But he had to finish another two labors before he would be pardoned. He retired to his house and waited for the next labor, which he knew would be another difficult one. Perhaps something that even he could not accomplish.

After eight months or so, the message arrived. He was to bring back the golden apples, which belonged to the great god Zeus. Hercules understood that Eurystheus wanted him to fail. Something belonging to Zeus, the king of gods, could not be touched, let alone stolen. Hera had given these apples as a wedding gift to Zeus, and Hercules was sure that Hera would not allow anyone to touch the apples.

The apples were in a garden towards the northern edge of the Earth, and were guarded at all times by a dragon called Ladon, who had a hundred heads! There were other guards too. The Nymphs, who were the daughters of the Titan who held up the sky—Atlas.

The problem that Hercules had to solve first was to locate the garden where the apples were. He did not know where the garden was. He started traveling and journeyed through several countries—Libya, Egypt, and Asia—but had no luck.

On his journey through these lands, Hercules came across Antaeus, a son of Poseidon, who challenged him to a fight. Hercules defeated Antaeus, crushing him. Next, another son of Poseidon stopped him, captured him, and took him to be offered as a human sacrifice, but Hercules managed to escape.

Then Hercules came to Mount Caucasus. Here he found Prometheus chained on a rock (on the orders of Zeus—remember?). The giant eagle that came to eat his liver every day was causing Prometheus a lot of pain. Hercules slew the eagle and released Prometheus.

Prometheus was grateful to Hercules and told him the location of the garden where the apples were kept. Prometheus also told Hercules that he would not be able to get the apples himself, but Atlas could get them for him if he could manage to convince him to help. Hercules first went to the garden and saw the tree with the golden apples. He tried to pick them from the branches, but every time he tried to touch an apple, it vanished. He then remembered what Prometheus had said. Abandoning his attempts at getting the apples, he went to see Atlas.

Atlas was tired of holding up the sky and jumped at the chance of shifting the load onto Hercules. He agreed to go get the apples for him. Hercules took over the task of holding up the sky while Atlas went to fetch the apples. But when Atlas came back with the apples, he did not want to hold up the sky and told Hercules to carry on holding it up in his place.

"I'll go and deliver them to Eurystheus for you!" said Atlas.

Hercules now had to think of a way to get out of this trap.

He told Atlas that he did not mind holding up the sky, but could Atlas take over for a minute while he used something to pad his shoulders? Atlas, unsuspecting, took over the load again. Hercules then picked up the apples and walked away, leaving Atlas to continue holding up the sky!

Arriving at Mycenae, Hercules showed the apples to Eurystheus and told him that they belonged to the gods and must be returned to them. Eurystheus knew that it was the truth and told Hercules to return them. Hercules went and handed over the apples to Athena, who in turn took them back to the garden. Hercules certainly must have thought wearily that after all the hard labor he went through to get the apples, they were now back in the garden! But he knew that he was safe from the curse of Zeus.

## CERBERUS (THE TWELFTH LABOR OF HERCULES)

Hercules, after the eleventh task, was awfully tired. He had traveled through many lands. There was also his narrow escape from the dreadful task of having to stay for the rest of his life holding up the sky. He thought of what the twelfth and last task would be. Eurystheus was sure to give him something that he would either fail to do or die trying. But he had no other option, so he waited.

By now, Eurystheus was thinking of something that Hercules could not do and then had an idea. He would ask Hercules to kidnap the beast called Cerberus who lived in the Underworld. The Underworld was ruled by Hades and his wife Persephone. Here, depending on what sort of deeds a person did while living, they would either be punished or rewarded. Good souls and bad souls—all went down to the Underworld. Hercules, he thought, would not dare to enter.

Cerberus was a fierce monster who guarded the gates of the Underworld so that no living thing could enter the world of the dead. Cerberus had three wild dog heads, a tail of serpent or dragon, and snakes covered his back. A weird but terrifying monster, as you can guess.

Hercules was wary of entering the Underworld. He knew that no living thing that entered ever came back. It was a one-way trip. He decided to first go to the priest Eumolpus, who was the keeper of secrets. Hercules needed protection before entering the Underworld. He approached Eumolpus and told him what he intended to do and asked for the protection of the Spirits. Eumolpus made Hercules go through several mystery rites before giving him what he wanted. He initiated Hercules into the Eleusinian Mysteries, which would serve to protect him when he reached the Underworld. Armed with divine protection, Hercules was now ready to enter.

Hercules knew that he could not just enter the Underworld through the main gate. That would be dangerous. He decided to enter through a side entrance, a rocky cave. As he entered, he met with many heroes, ghosts, and even monsters. But Hercules was brave and continued on his way into the Underworld. Then, he was confronted by the god Hades himself. Hades asked him what he wanted. Hercules told him about his tasks and that he wanted to take Cerberus with him, alive, to Mycenae. Hades agreed to allow Hercules to take Cerberus with him, but only if he could defeat Cerberus with his bare hands, without using any weapons. Hercules, confident of his strength, agreed and went in search of Cerberus.

Hercules found Cerberus near the gates and, using his strong arms, grasped the monster's three heads and held on tight. Cerberus fought with all his might but could not get out of the grip, although the dragon in his tail continuously bit Hercules. Finally, a weary Cerberus surrendered to Hercules, who took him to Eurystheus.

There is an end to this story. As Cerberus guarded the gates of the Underworld, he had to be returned. Hercules took Cerberus back and released him unharmed, exactly as he had promised the lord of the Underworld.

This task ended the labors of Hercules and he was pardoned for his sin. He was a free man after this. But besides these famous labors, Hercules had many exciting adventures, some of which you will now discover. He was a restless sort of person and he could not stay home and was always looking for something exciting to do.

## THE OTHER ADVENTURES OF HERCULES

As Hercules was wandering around, he heard that Eurytus, the ruler of Oechalia, was offering his beautiful daughter Iole in marriage to anyone who could defeat him and his sons in a contest of archery. Hearing this, Hercules went to Oechalia and defeated the ruler and his sons in the contest. But the king went back on his promise and refused to allow Hercules to marry his daughter. Hercules was annoyed and went away, very angry. But one of the sons of Eurytus, Iphytus, did not agree with his father's actions and went in search of Hercules.

Hercules was resting when Iphytus found him. They sat together and drank and ate and made merry. But then something happened between them, and Hercules, in a fit of rage, killed Iphytus. This was a bad thing to have done, and days later Hercules developed a peculiar disease that he could not cure. He realized that the only way was to go to the Oracle of Delphi and ask for a cure. This Oracle of Delphi was a temple with a priestess who would deliver prophecies. Everyone who went there followed the advice of the oracle.

Hercules went to the temple and asked for a cure. But the oracle refused to tell him anything. Enraged, Hercules started destroying the temple. He took the sacred tripod (known as the Delphic Tripod) from the temple and wanted to carry it away with him. This alarmed the gods. Apollo intervened and began to fight with Hercules. Both were powerful and the fight grew serious. Zeus now saw that it was time he intervened to stop this nonsense. He threw a thunderbolt that separated the two combatants. The tripod was replaced and the priestess then sent forth an oracle. Hercules was to spend one year in slavery. He was given to Queen Omphale (one of the many minor characters in the myths), and there he completed his punishment. The story shows that too much pride and anger are not good and inevitably lead to bad things.

Hercules was also involved in the battle against the Giants. These were ferocious monsters who were as tall as the mountains. These monsters decided to attack Olympus, the place where the gods lived. Zeus knew that he needed the help of Hercules because the Giants were very dangerous enemies. Hercules came and took part in the battle, killing several of the Giants.

Hercules then got involved in another adventure. He told Laomedon, King of Ilium, that he would rescue his daughter, Hesione, from her fate. Hesione was tied to a rock as an offering to the gods to prevent an epidemic. She was to be devoured by a dragon! When the dragon arrived to eat her, Hercules killed it. But again, as had happened many times in his life, the king refused to reward Hercules, going back on his word. Hercules came back with six ships, attacked Laomedon, and killed him and his sons in revenge. He then gave Hesione in marriage to one of his friends.

# CHAPTER 4: THE OLYMPIANS

Greek mythology has many gods and goddesses, too numerous to talk about. But in this chapter, we shall talk about the more important ones. The gods and goddesses had big impacts and ruled over important parts of the universe.

## ZEUS

Zeus was the most important god of the Greeks. He was the son of Cronus and Rhea, though Zeus grew up away from his parents. He was an important god and we shall see that he is perhaps the most important god in all of Greek mythology, as he makes an appearance or is mentioned in almost every myth. He was in fact the king of kings! Although other gods ruled over different parts of the universe, Zeus was master overall. His word was final in all matters. He punished any god who disobeyed him. Remember Prometheus? Greek myth is full of the activities of Zeus. He was the one who would decide the fate of the other gods whenever there was a dispute.

## POSEIDON

Zeus was the most powerful ruler, but Poseidon, who was his brother, was of no less importance. He was given rulership over the seas and the oceans, and that is quite a lot to rule over.

When Zeus fought the Titans and the Giants, Poseidon fought alongside him.

Poseidon was also known as the god of earthquakes and horses. The trident that he carried had the power to shake the Earth whenever Poseidon threw it down on the ground. Poseidon lived deep in the ocean in a fantastic palace surrounded by sea creatures and monsters.

Whenever he traveled, he fastened his chariot to swift horses with golden manes and bronze hooves. He dressed in golden armor and traveled across the oceans, which parted to let him through. As he swept through the waves, sea monsters came up to pay homage to their ruler. You can imagine the sight of this chariot racing through the seas and sea monsters rising up. An impressive sight indeed! In most Greek paintings, you will see Poseidon with long unruly hair and carrying his famous trident. He was quite a scary-looking character.

## APOLLO

The exact origin of this important god is not very clear. Apollo was always depicted as a handsome young man, slim and strong. He was said to have ruled over sunlight. As you know, the heat of sunlight is needed to ripen crops and fruit. As a result, Apollo also had rulership over harvests. Accordingly, when people harvested their first grain they made an offering to Apollo, to make the god happy, and ensure that the next harvest was also good. In many cultures, offering the first harvest to the gods is still practiced.

Apollo's mother was Leto. When Apollo was just an infant, he showed that he was not an ordinary god. There was a serpent called Python, who was evil. Apollo decided to kill him. He took with him the arrows fashioned by Hephaestus, the master craftsman, and traveled to Parnassus, where the serpent lived. When the serpent saw him, it attacked. But Apollo hit him with an arrow. The serpent fell to the ground and began moaning in pain. Apollo looked at the serpent with contempt and said "lie there and rot, evil creature."

Apollo was also a shepherd god, looking after the flocks of cattle, sheep, and other domesticated animals. He was important to people who kept cattle and they prayed to him so that their herds were always safe from predators.

Music and song were also said to be Apollo's domain. He was often shown with a lyre in his hands. It was said that the gods often listened to Apollo singing and playing the lyre. Since music and song were always important, he had a very important portfolio. How he got the lyre is in another story that you will read about soon.

He was also known as the Celestial Archer. His arrows never missed their mark.

Apollo, however, was still a very strong god. As you will see, he did not shy away from a fight. In Phocis, there was a man called Phorbas (a mortal), who had extraordinary strength and who waylaid people going to the temple of Delphi and made them fight him. Because he was very strong, he defeated them. He would then torture them and kill them. Apollo decided to put a stop to this bandit. He disguised himself as an athlete and appeared on the road to Delphi. Phorbas challenged Apollo to a fight and Apollo felled him with one mighty blow of his fist. Phorbas had made the mistake of challenging the wrong person!

When Hercules went mad and started destroying the temple of the Delphic Oracle, Apollo fought with him. Hercules, as you know, was known as someone who had superhuman strength, but Apollo did not shy away from fighting him.

He had much respect in the king's council. All the gods honored him when he came in. Even Zeus respected Apollo.

## HERMES

Hermes ruled over several things. It is said that he ruled over travelers and ensured safe passage to those who prayed to him. In those days, travel was mostly for business so Hermes automatically became the god of commerce. He is also said to have ruled the wind. His rulership is not very clear in the myths.

One thing is for sure, Hermes was the messenger for Zeus, delivering his messages to mortals and gods alike. And Zeus always kept sending messages to various gods.

Hermes wore winged sandals when he was delivering messages for Zeus. Sometimes he also wore a hat with wings to aid in his travels through the skies.

The son of Zeus and Meia, Hermes was born in a cave. It is said that on the day of his birth he showed his mischievous nature by stealing cattle that belonged to Apollo. You might think—a newborn baby? Babies can't even get up! But we are talking about gods, remember?

Hermes quietly climbed out of his cradle and snuck out. He then climbed the mountain of Pieria where the sacred herd was kept. He took 50 heads of cattle from the herd and drove them under the cover of darkness to a place called Alpheus. Hermes was so clever that he made them walk backward, so that nobody would know which way they had gone. He put on big sandals so that his footprints would make everyone think the thief was a grown man! He hid the cattle in a cavern, but he wasn't finished yet. He selected two of the fattest heifers and roasted them. He divided up the meat into 12 equal portions and offered the food to the 12 gods. After that, he turned himself into vapor, re-entered his room through a keyhole, and lay down in his cradle again.

Apollo discovered his loss, and by using his divine powers, realized that Hermes was the culprit. In a rage, he went to the cave where Hermes lay and accused him. "Why did you steal my cattle?" Hermes looked up innocently at Apollo and denied having taken the cattle.

Apollo then picked him up and took him to Zeus for judgment. Zeus was amused and could not but praise the ingenuity of Hermes. But he also knew that Apollo was a god and would not tolerate disrespect. He told Hermes to return the cattle to Apollo. Hermes showed them where the cattle were and Apollo got them back.

Zeus and the other Olympians in the court were entranced by this bubbly child who seemed extremely clever. Hephaestus, who was present at the court, was taken in by the charm that Hermes displayed, sitting on Zeus's lap and fiddling with the god's beard.

All the gods decided that Hermes must become the divine messenger.

Hephaestus decided to give him a gift and made a pair of sandals that had wings. These sandals would allow Hermes to literally zip through the sky to any place that he wanted to go. Grateful for the gift, Hermes gave Hephaestus a great big hug of joy. Hephaestus was not used to being hugged. He was ugly and not many people hugged or touched him. He was so overcome with happiness that he went back to his forge and made a helmet with wings and gave that to Hermes too. This helmet would make Hermes faster through the air. Hephaestus also gave Hermes a silver staff with two snakes entwined on the top.

However, Hermes knew that Apollo was still angry. He had not yet forgotten the taking of his cattle by Hermes. Hermes decided to make amends and made a stringed instrument (later known as a lyre) using the shell of a turtle, and went to meet Apollo. But Apollo was annoyed and showed it until Hermes started playing the lyre. The celestial sound of the instrument delighted Apollo. Hermes knew that Apollo wanted it, but could not ask for it. So he gave it to Apollo as a gift. Apollo now forgot all his anger and he and Hermes became lifelong friends. Apollo entrusted Hermes with the care of the celestial herd.

Apollo became the god of music, as he was always playing the lyre and singing, and Hermes became the protector of flocks and herds. Hermes was part of many adventures and helped many mortals and gods overcome their problems.

## ARES

Greek myths say Ares is the god of war and strife. Zeus did not like him and one day in the Council of the gods, Zeus told Ares that he disliked him the most because all he did was enjoy battles, strife, and war. Ares did not mind because he knew that he was the god of war. Somebody had to be.

Ares used to roam around mounted on a chariot that was drawn by swift horses with golden browbands. He himself was clad in bronze armor, with a mighty spear in his hand. He went around battlefields and struck blows on either side. He did not care who was fighting whom or for what reason. He just entered into the battle and fought.

Ares, however, was a very brutal and bloodthirsty god, who was never happier unless he was killing or fighting someone. This made everyone dislike him and even the gods avoided him. But Ares did not always win whatever battle he was fighting. Most often he came away wounded and defeated. Hercules once beat him up and he ran away to Olympus to lick his wounds. Ares got into many difficulties and sticky situations because of his liking for trouble.

## HEPHAESTUS

Remember Hephaestus? He was the god from whom Prometheus stole fire and gave it to mankind.

Hephaestus, although a god, was not very good-looking. He was lame in both legs, which meant that they were deformed. His feet were twisted and he walked at a stumbling pace. The other gods were mean and laughed at his peculiar walk.

Hera, the mother of Hephaestus, was so ashamed of his disfigured body that she threw him into the sea, where he remained under the care of Thetis, another goddess. Later, he was reunited with his mother.

Hephaestus was a master craftsman of metals. He had a forge where he made magical items for the gods. He was extremely inventive, and the gods came to him when they needed something made out of metal. Things like swords, armor, and shields, which the gods always needed, as there was always some war or battle happening somewhere.

Hephaestus may have been ugly, but he was a genius with metals. He made for himself a palace of bronze, which was said to be indestructible. Inside this palace, he had his forge, where he could be seen hammering red hot metal into various objects. He is said to have created many palaces of bronze for the gods. Whenever a god came to see him, he would clean himself up (as he was working with fire and therefore always sweating) and then go and sit on his throne. He would then ask whichever god or goddess had come what they wanted. He knew that he was the best.

Among his famous creations are the golden throne, a scepter and thunderbolts for Zeus, arrows for Apollo and Artemis, a cuirass for Hercules, and armor for Achilles (who was an important figure in the great battle between the Greeks and the Trojans called the Trojan War).

Hephaestus always did whatever Zeus asked him to do. It was he who created the chains to bind Prometheus to the rock. He did it against his will because he knew that to annoy Zeus was dangerous.

Hephaestus, however, had not forgotten the treatment by his mother. She had not been a good mother to him and had cast him away down a mountainside and into the sea. He decided to take revenge. He built a magnificent throne of gold and sent it as an anonymous gift to his mother Hera.

Hera was fascinated by the throne and sat down on it. Immediately, the arms of the throne closed in and trapped her. She could not get up! Everyone rushed in to free her, but to no avail. Even Zeus failed. A while later, Hephaestus arrived. He pretended he did not know about Hera's problem. He casually asked if Hera was trapped on the throne. Hera, who was terrified and annoyed, said, "can't you see that I am trapped on this infernal throne!"

Hephaestus went towards her and the throne released its grip, freeing Hera. Hephaestus was then treated with respect by Hera. She realized that her son was indeed a special person.

## ATHENA

Athena was known for her valor in the field of battle. Athena liked and protected the brave. She helped Hercules when he was busy finishing the labors given to him by Eurystheus. When Hercules was given the labor of driving away from the Stymphalian birds, he was puzzled. He had no idea how to drive away such a large flock of birds. It was Athena who gave him the clappers. These were special clappers designed by Hephaestus that made such a loud sound that Hercules easily drove the birds away.

Athena had a benevolent side to her character and during times when she was not engaged in battle, she did many useful things. She taught the people of Cyrene to tame horses. She also helped Jason to design and build the ship Argo.

One of her important inventions was her designing and building the first potter's wheel, which was used by the people to make vases and other earthen pots. At the time, this was a great help. These pots and vases were used to store grain, water, and other things. The potter's wheel is still used today.

Athena also taught the women the fine art of weaving and embroidery. If there was no weaving, there would be no clothes today, would there?

There is a particularly interesting and intriguing story about Athena.

In a place called Lydia, there lived a girl called Arachne. This girl was known for her skill in using the needle and spindle. One day she took it into her head to challenge Athena to compete with her. Athena was angry that a mere mortal dared challenge her. She wanted to punish Arachne but instead accepted the challenge. She, Athena, was the goddess who invented the process, after all. She sent word that she was ready for the challenge.

Athena went to meet Arachne disguised as an old woman.

"Withdraw your challenge to Athena. She is a goddess. How dare you challenge her?" she said. Arachne refused to back down.

Athena then took on her divine form, blazing with light, and told Arachne that she accepted the challenge.

Arachne immediately sat on her loom and started weaving. She used colored threads and used, as her design, the loves of the gods. When she finished she offered it to Athena for inspection.

Athena carefully inspected the cloth, but try as she might, she could not find a single flaw. Enraged, she cursed Arachne and turned her into a spider.

"You shall spend the rest of your days weaving using the thread from your own body!" said Athena.

Spiders still use their body fluid to weave their webs. The next time you see a spider, it could be Arachne! What do you think? It's still a myth after all—a story, right? Or is it?

## APHRODITE

Aphrodite is the goddess of love and beauty. She was born from the sea and was so beautiful that all the other goddesses were jealous of her. They decided to ask someone, a mortal, to judge who was the most beautiful. The contestants were Hera, Athena, and of course, Aphrodite.

The gods decided that Paris, the son of King Priam of Troy would be the judge. All three goddesses descended on Troy. Paris was tending to his flocks along a hillside when the three goddesses presented themselves. When Paris heard what they wanted him to do, he refused. Paris was clever, he did not want to get involved with goddesses. He knew that if he chose one of them, the others would bear him a grudge, and he could do without grudges from goddesses.

The three goddesses, however, insisted and said that Zeus had made the decision for them to come to him. This time Paris had no choice. The two goddesses, Hera and Athena, promised him land and kingdoms if he chose them.

Only Aphrodite did not offer Paris anything. She had nothing much to offer. But Paris was so struck by her dazzling beauty that he chose her. Aphrodite was the winner.

Hera and Athena were not pleased and later they would avenge this insult by creating the Trojan War in which Paris was killed, and the kingdom of Troy was devastated by the Greeks.

You must have read about the Trojan horse. It was actually a Greek horse. The Greeks hid inside the giant wooden horse and left it outside Troy. The Trojans unknowingly took the horse inside their fortress. The Greeks jumped out of the horse and defeated the Trojans. The Greeks also destroyed the city of Troy. The goddesses had their revenge.

## HESTIA

The Greek word *Hestia* means 'hearth.' In those days, it meant the place where the fire was kept burning. Nowadays people light a fire when they need it, but remember that in ancient times, a fire was a precious thing. Prometheus risked his life to bring it to the humans. Therefore, a fire was always tended to and looked after, and treated with respect. In those days you didn't just have matches.

When a member of a family went away to set up a new home, he took with him the family fire, so that the continuity of the family was maintained. People also made a place in the community where a public fire was kept burning. Hestia was the goddess of all these fires.

Hestia was also the fire in which men sacrificed things to the gods. Hestia was not a goddess who had many adventures but being the keeper of the household fires, she was still important. In ancient Greece, a fire was a very valuable commodity.

# CHAPTER 5: IMPORTANT HEROES (PART 1)

## THESEUS

Theseus was like Hercules. He was very strong and went about destroying monsters. It is said that when he was still a child, he attacked the body of the Nemean lion, although it was already dead. Hercules had killed it and left the body on a table. Grown, Theseus began getting rid of several bad people who preyed on the innocent.

He heard that Sinis, a son of Poseidon, was torturing anyone who came his way. Sinis would tie the person between two bent pine trees and then release the trees so that the person was torn apart. Theseus decided to punish Sinis and went to see him. Sinis, thinking that Theseus was just another man, tried to hurt him. Theseus, who was also the son of Poseidon, killed him.

One of the great exploits of Theseus was the killing of the Minotaur, a creature with the body of a man and the head of a bull.

The son of Minos, the ruler of Crete, was killed by the Athenians. Minos exacted revenge by sending his ambassadors to Athens to fetch seven young men and seven maidens. These were to be fed to the Minotaur, which Minos kept prisoner in a labyrinth. This labyrinth was made by the very clever craftsman Daedalus (we shall be talking about him later). The Minotaur was a fierce creature and would kill and devour the 14 young men and women. This was going on for years.

However, Theseus was in Athens when the ambassadors came to collect the 14 unfortunate young men and women. Theseus was angry and decided to go with the youth and kill the creature. When he arrived at Crete, he met Minos.

"And who are you?" asked Minos. Theseus replied that he was the son of Poseidon.

Minos did not believe him. "Well, if you really are the son of Poseidon, then fetch me this," said Minos, and he threw a golden ring into the sea.

Theseus dived into the sea and returned with the ring.

But by this time a daughter of Minos, Ariadne, had fallen in love with Theseus and decided to help him. She knew that the labyrinth was a difficult place to get out of, as it was so cleverly constructed by Daedalus. It was made this way to keep the Minotaur from getting out.

"Take this ball of string with you, so that you can find your way out of the labyrinth. Tie it to a tree when you go in and let the string unwind as you go. Once you have killed the Minotaur, follow the string back out," Ariadne told Theseus.

Theseus used the string exactly as Ariadne had told him to do, and after killing the Minotaur he followed the string and got out of the labyrinth.

Among his other exploits, he went with Hercules to get the belt from Hippolyte, the queen of the Amazons. He was the one who warned Hercules that the Amazons were preparing to attack.

Theseus was bored one day and thought that he would get rid of the bandits who tortured travelers. That, he felt, would bring him glory. He had already punished Sinis.

So he took off on foot with his sword and a few things in a bag.

The first bandit he met was giant cyclops named Periphetes. He was carrying a huge club.

"What's in the bag?" he asked Theseus.

When Theseus did not reply, the giant began to get angry.

"I am going to smash your head with my bronze club!" he said.

However, Theseus was clever. "That club is not made of bronze, it is made of wood. Anyone can see that."

The cyclops was angry at hearing this and offered Theseus the club to see if it was made of bronze or not. "See if you can hold it."

Theseus pretended that it was heavy and, gripping the club, hit the giant on its legs. The giant fell to the ground in pain. Theseus then hit him several times and finally killed him. He then went on his way, taking the club with him.

As he moved further on his journey, he came across a menacing bad character called Sciron. Theseus knew what Sciron did. He took people to the top of a cliff. There, he asked them to sit on the edge of the cliff with their backs to the sea and wash their feet. When the victim was doing this, Sciron would kick the man into the sea, where a giant turtle would eat him. As soon as Sciron saw Theseus, he approached him and pointed a sword at him.

"Wash my feet or die!" said Sciron, but Theseus was ready.

"I don't want to. Your feet are dirty and smelly," replied Theseus, standing calmly.

"Either you wash my feet, or I kill you now," said Sciron, pressing the sword point harder into Theseus's body.

Theseus pretended to consider and then said that he needed hot water, oils, and cloth to properly wash Sciron's feet.

The bandit agreed and brought Theseus his hot water, oils, and cloth.

As he began to wash the feet of Sciron, he was pushed right to the edge of the cliff. Theseus suddenly pretended to lose his balance and stumbled against Sciron. He then threw the hot water into the bandit's face, blinding him.

One hefty shove and Sciron was hurtling down on his way into the sea. The turtle was waiting for prey and probably ate Sciron.

The last major adventure of Theseus was to destroy a couple who offered hospitality and then tortured the guest. If the guest was tall, they would reduce the size of the bed. They would then ask the guest to lie down. When the legs of the guest dangled over the edge of the bed, Procrustes would cut them off, saying that the guest was too tall for the bed. The bed had a mechanism to make it longer or shorter. When the guest was short, Procrustes would lengthen the bed and tell the guest that he was too short. They would then use the mechanism of the bed to stretch the guest. Either way, the guests died in agony. Theseus did not know this, but when Procrustes, who was the host, invited Theseus into the hostelry, Theseus became suspicious. He saw that the wife of Procrustes was inside making food, and the two exchanged glances.

Theseus said that he would like to take a bath, and went out to the pond behind the house. However, he did not go to the pond. He circled back to the window and overheard them talking about how they were going to torture him before killing him. Theseus pretended not to know and after dinner, went to lie down. Procrustes went with him. Theseus then threw Procrustes onto the bed. Theseus gave Procrustes a dose of his own medicine. In this way, Theseus ended the terrible deeds of Procrustes and his wife.

## JASON OF THE ARGONAUTS

This myth or story is also sometimes called "Jason and the Golden Fleece." As we shall see, the Golden Fleece does play an important part.

It is one of the oldest myths where a hero goes on a quest. It is a story of adventure and betrayal. But before we begin, you must know why Jason went in search of the Golden Fleece.

The chain of events began when Pelias killed Jason's father, the king of Iolcus, and usurped the throne. Jason's mother, afraid that Pelias might kill the infant Jason too, took him to a centaur called Chiron, who was half-man and half-horse. Chiron carried the infant Jason away and raised him.

Meanwhile, Pelias ruled Iolcus with a tyrannical hand, crushing any form of dissent and protest. He was an oppressive ruler, someone who ruled by the use of brute force. Nobody could remove him as he was so vicious in his vengeance. Pelias was very vigilant because an oracle had prophesied that his throne would be taken from him by a relative wearing one sandal, and his spies were instructed to keep a sharp eye out for such a person.

Meanwhile, Jason had slowly grown up and reached the age of 20. Chiron, who was taking care of Jason, taught him the secrets of herbs and medicines, but realized that Jason was more of an athletic and physical sort of boy.

Chiron then told Jason about his father, and how Pelias had treacherously killed him and taken away the throne. Jason vowed revenge but bided his time. He had learned the benefits of patience from Chiron.

The day came when Jason decided he would travel to Iolcus and demand his rights. He would ask Pelias to give him the throne that was now rightfully his.

He bid Chiron adieu and started on his journey.

Jason walked for days and came to a river—not a deep one, but a river nevertheless. On the bank, he saw an old woman, who was bent over double. He offered to carry her on his back across the river. Hoisting her onto his back, Jason entered the river and began wading through to the opposite side. The old woman on his back kept clawing at him and muttering something.

When he reached the other side, he realized that one of his sandals had come off, and was stuck in some rocks in the river. He tried to wade back in to retrieve the sandal, but the old woman kept clawing at him. By the time he managed to free himself from her hands, the sandal had been washed away. Jason realized that he would have to continue with only one sandal. Meanwhile, he saw that the old lady had vanished without a trace.

The old lady was in fact Hera, a goddess, who wanted to help Jason in his fight against Pelias, whom she hated. Why she hated him is another story, and Hera hated a lot of people anyway. For now, we go with Jason.

When Jason arrived at Iolcus, he wandered around looking at everything. People started staring at this handsome stranger. They were intrigued by the fact that he was only wearing one sandal.

The palace guards ran to Pelias to inform him of the presence of Jason. Of course, they did not know his name as of yet. But the king had to be informed.

Pelias was busy with his own work when the guards arrived.

"Stranger? What kind of stranger?" he asked the guards.

"He is tall with long golden hair. He is wearing the skin of a lion, my Lord!" replied the guard.

Pelias began to think. Who was this golden-haired stranger now?

One of the guards remembered something. "He walks with a limp, my Lord."

"With a limp?" Pelias asked, now more mystified.

The other guard, however, was more observant. "He limps because he is wearing just one sandal."

Pelias now sat up straight. "Wearing just one sandal? Are you sure?"

The guards nodded vigorously.

"Bring him here. I want to meet him," he commanded, beginning to feel uneasy. Was this the one who would take away his throne? The prophecy began to haunt him.

"Wait. I think I will go out and meet him. Where is he now?" asked Pelias.

"He is in the marketplace, my Lord," said one of the guards.

Pelias hurried out to meet this unusual stranger, who wore just one sandal.

Arriving at the marketplace, he found Jason surrounded by admirers. He also saw that the stranger was indeed wearing just one sandal.

Seeing the king, most of the folk made way.

Pelias approached Jason and asked who he was.

Jason believed in the direct approach and said, "I have come to demand what is mine, Uncle."

Pelias was a little taken aback. *Uncle?* Pelias did have a lot of nephews. Then the thought struck him. Here was a relative wearing one sandal! Was this the man the prophecy had spoken about? But Pelias was a devious and cunning man and was determined not to give up his throne so easily.

"So nephew, what is your name?" he asked in a friendly manner.

"I am Jason, son of Aeson, the former king of Iolcus. You killed my father and usurped the throne. I am the rightful heir to the throne and have come to take back what is mine."

Hearing these words, Pelias knew that the past had come back to haunt him. He had to figure out a way to thwart the prophecy from being fulfilled. He thought quickly.

Pelias put his hand around Jason's shoulders and said that he would willingly give up the kingdom to Jason, but there was a problem. The kingdom was cursed.

Jason had not heard of any curse, so he asked Pelias to explain.

Pelias then began to explain the details of the curse to Jason.

Pelias said that he had consulted an oracle when he noticed that there was no peace and prosperity in his kingdom, and the oracle had informed him that the Golden Fleece must be brought back. It must be brought back by the king to Iolcus. After that, the kingdom would be prosperous. This was a total fib. Pelias had done no such thing.

He then continued with his false tale. He asked Jason whether he had heard of his cousin Phrixus. Jason admitted knowing his cousin Phrixus.

Pelias then told Jason that his cousin had died in a place called Colchis, and had kept the Golden Fleece there. As the new king of Iolcus, Jason must be the one to bring back the Golden Fleece from Colchis. The oracle was firm on that point. The king had to personally go and fetch the Golden Fleece. Only then would the curse be lifted.

Jason considered this and decided to go on this quest for the benefit of the people.

"It shall be done, Uncle! I shall go and bring the Golden Fleece here to Iolcus," said Jason, who was happy that he had a grand quest to go on at last.

Pelias was beside himself with glee. He knew that the task was beset by problems and chances were that Jason would not come back alive. The Golden Fleece was guarded by a fierce dragon that never slept, and just getting there was fraught with danger.

Before we continue, it is important to know how the Golden Fleece came to be in Colchis.

Zeus had given a golden ram to Phrixus (Jason's cousin). Phrixus sat on the ram and flew to Colchis from Greece. Colchis was ruled by a king named Aeetes, who was the son of Helios, the sun god.

Aeetes sacrificed the ram to Zeus and hung the golden fleece in a sacred garden, and put a dragon there to guard it. This was the creature that never slept. Since the ram was a gift from Zeus, the fleece too was a valuable object.

That in short is the story of the Golden Fleece.

Now back to Jason, who was planning his trip to bring back this valuable object.

Jason knew that Colchis was far away and he needed a very good ship to sail in. He approached Argus, an expert shipbuilder. The vessel he built was very strong and had excellent sails and rowing equipment. It was named the Argo in his honor. And yes, you guessed it—the men who sailed in it came to be known as the Argonauts!

Once the ship was ready, Jason announced that he needed heroes to sail to Colchis. Several great warriors came and joined. Hercules, too, joined. He had some time in between his labors and found the idea exciting.

Jason now had a great crew and he set sail. The first port of call was the Isle of Lemnos. Jason did not know that the Isle was populated only by women, who were known as Amazons. They had been sent away from their men and lived by themselves. Jason, however, cleverly managed to leave the Isle without getting into trouble with the women who lived there. (Pelias was sure that when Argonauts reached Lemnos, the women would not allow them to leave. Maybe even kill them. But he was wrong.)

Next, they had to cross the treacherous straits of Bosphorus. The straits were narrow watery passages, and there were rocks on either side of the passage that slammed shut when any vessel tried to pass through, crushing the vessel and killing everyone. Jason was warned of this by an old blind man whom he had helped. The blind man told Jason about a trick he could use to get through the straits without being crushed.

Jason, following the old man's advice, released a dove. The dove flew through the straits and the rocks closed in, but the dove managed to fly through. The old man had told Jason that if the dove could fly through, they too would be able to sail successfully and cross the straits. As soon as the rocks opened, Jason ordered the crew to row as fast as they could. The Argo swept through the straits before the rocks could crush it.

Finally, the Argonauts arrived at Colchis. Jason went to meet King Aeetes, who, although a little surprised to see so many great warriors visiting his kingdom, welcomed them warmly. He thought that they were just passing by. He was wrong.

Jason told the king that he had come to take the Golden Fleece, as it originally belonged to his ancestor Phrixus. The king thought for a moment and told Jason that he was quite willing to give the Golden Fleece to Jason. Secretly, he considered killing Jason and his band of men but realized that other gods and heroes might come back and destroy him in revenge. Besides, the gods might be angry and punish him. The king, exactly like Pelias, now decided to lie. He had a plan that might prevent Jason from leaving with the Fleece.

He called Jason to come close and said, "long ago I prayed to the gods for guidance about the Golden Fleece. The gods told me that the Fleece could be taken only by someone prepared to undertake three tasks and complete them successfully."

Jason believed the king and said that he was ready to perform the three tasks. But the king was not done yet.

"The tasks have to be completed by you and you alone. Your men cannot help you in any way," said Aeetes, trying to ensure that Jason would fail.

Jason nodded his head. He had no other choice. He asked for the details of the three tasks.

The first task was to harness two bulls that had mouths and hooves of bronze and breathed fire and use them to plow a field. These bulls were well-known. They were called The Oxen of Colchis, or the Khalkotauroi. They were fierce creatures and nobody went near them.

"And the second task?" asked Jason.

"I have some dragon teeth that must be planted in the furrows made by the plow. Once you do this, armed men will rise from the ground. You will have to fight and defeat them," said Aeetes with a smile. He was going to make it as difficult as he could.

"The third task is to kill the dragon that guards the Fleece and is coiled around the tree, on which the Fleece hangs," said Aeetes.

Jason wearily agreed but sighed in frustration.

However, the gods Athena and Hera were listening and they decided to help Jason. They asked Aphrodite, the goddess of love, to make Medea, the daughter of King Aeetes, fall in love with Jason. Medea was adept at all sorts of potions and spells. She had been trained by Hecate, another goddess. Once she fell in love with Jason, she would assist him.

At night when Jason was roaming around in the palace, Medea came to him and told him that she was in love with him, and would help him complete the three tasks.

She gave Jason an ointment and told him to smear it all over his body. This would make him invincible.

The next day, the king, queen, and their daughters and son were present to see Jason begin his tasks.

Jason waited for the bulls to be released. The gates were opened and two fierce bulls emerged, breathing fire. Jason waited patiently for the bulls to come to him. He had his sword and shield ready. But in his hands, he had a yoke, which was a wooden piece that fastened animals to plows, and a harness.

The bulls charged him, but Jason did not move. He hit one of the bulls with his shield and stabbed the other one with his sword. The ointment given by Medea saved him from the fire that the bulls were throwing at him.

Slowly, the bulls tired and Jason fastened them to the plow. But as soon as he had plowed the field and planted the dragon's teeth, giant warriors began to emerge from the ground. However, Medea had told him that the best way to defeat these warriors was to throw a large rock into their midst. Jason picked up a large boulder and tossed it. It landed on two of the warriors. Strangely enough, the warriors then began to fight amongst themselves. They killed each other until a single warrior was left standing. Jason walked up to him and cut off his head with one slice of his sword. He had finished his second task. The crowd who had gathered to witness this spectacle were now cheering Jason on, and King Aeetes was scared.

Jason was now ready for the last task: Defeating the dragon and taking the Golden Fleece.

Jason entered the garden where the Golden Fleece was kept and saw the dragon wound around the tree. Medea, who had gone with Jason, put a spell on the dragon and it became paralyzed. Medea then placed a concoction of flowers and herbs into its mouth and it fell asleep. Jason reached out and took the Golden Fleece. Together, Jason and Medea went to the ship that was waiting for them and they set sail for Iolcus.

Jason took over the kingship of Iolcus and ruled for some years happily.

Jason's story is rather long, but is worth reading, as it has several smaller stories in it. Greek myth is sometimes quite complex, with many smaller plots interwoven. But the stories, whether small or big, are all fascinating.

# CHAPTER 6: IMPORTANT HEROES (PART 2)

## DAEDALUS AND ICARUS

Daedalus, if you remember, was a god and a master craftsman. He designed and built many palaces for kings. He had designed a complex labyrinth for King Minos. In this labyrinth, Minos kept the Minotaur imprisoned. Anybody who went in could never get out, so cleverly was it designed.

Daedalus and Minos were great friends, but slowly, Minos began to dislike Daedalus. Nobody is quite sure why their friendship suddenly turned sour, but Minos began to hate Daedalus.

Daedalus had with him his son Icarus, a young boy who he loved very much.

At some point, Minos was so angry with Daedalus that he took him and his son Icarus and placed them in the labyrinth. Daedalus knew that they would never be able to get out on foot. Daedalus knew that the labyrinth was too complicated, he had, after all, designed and built it himself. Daedalus also knew that the seaports would be watched by Minos's soldiers. There was only one way to escape—by air.

Daedalus began to think. Then he got an idea. He would develop artificial wings for himself and his son and they would fly away to freedom. He set about his task immediately. Using branches from the plants in the labyrinth, he wove them into wings. Now the question was: How to fix the wings onto the body?

Daedalus decided to use wax. He melted the wax and attached the wings to his body. He then did the same for Icarus. They tried to flap the wings first to see if they would work. They did, so Daedalus and Icarus decided to fly out of the labyrinth together.

When they were ready, they both flapped their wings and flew out of the labyrinth and started flying away from Crete. They flew over the sea and everything was working well, until Icarus, with his youthful energy, started flying up and then down. Daedalus realized the danger at once and warned Icarus not to fly too close to the sun, as the heat of the sun's rays would melt the wax and the wings would come off. But Icarus was having too much fun to care. He kept swooping down to the sea and then up again. What Daedalus had feared happened then. Icarus flew too close to the sun and the wax melted. His wings came off and he fell into the sea and drowned. Daedalus managed to get away safely. This story is a little tragic, but it does not end here.

King Minos was enraged when he discovered that Daedalus and his son Icarus had escaped with the help of artificial wings. He decided to find Daedalus and punish him. But where would he find Daedalus? He could be anywhere. Suddenly, an idea came to him. He took a conch shell and set sail. He let it be known that anyone who could thread the shell would be given huge riches as a prize. That meant that the thread had to be inserted at one end and taken out the other.

He sailed from city to city and many people tried to thread the shell without success. Minos knew that only the clever Daedalus would be able to do it. At last, he arrived at the city of Camicus. King Cocalus was interested in the challenge and took the shell from Minos. He took it to Daedalus, who looked at the shell for a minute. Then he got an ant and tied the thread to it. Using honey, he lured the ant through the curvature of the shell until it came out at the other end.

King Cocalus handed the threaded shell to Minos, who immediately knew that Daedalus had done it and that he was there. Minos threatened King Cocalus with a full-blown invasion if he did not hand over Daedalus. The king asked for a moment and went in to consult his daughters. His daughters, when they heard what had happened, drew up a plan.

Cocalus went to Minos and told him that Daedalus would be handed over to him the next day, and meanwhile, he should have a bath and eat a hearty meal. Minos accepted the offer. But when he entered the bathtub, the daughters, trained by Daedalus, introduced very hot water into the pipes. The pipes burst with the pressure and Minos was scalded and killed. The whole thing was passed off as an accident and no one was blamed. Daedalus was safe.

## OEDIPUS AND THE SPHINX

Oedipus was an abandoned child adopted and brought up by a king and queen. They were not his real parents but raised him with all the benefits of royalty.

Oedipus loved to wander around. He would walk for miles and live frugally. One afternoon, he found himself in the countryside, near the town of Daulis. He found that he was at a crossroads, with three roads going three different ways. He stood undecided when down one road a chariot came speeding at him. The old coachman shouted and cracked his whip at him to get out of the way. Oedipus grabbed his whip and threw him off the coach. When the coach stopped, four armed men got out and came for Oedipus. But Oedipus managed to kill three of them before the fourth fled for his life. He then tore off a branch from an olive tree and started pulling off the leaves, saying the words, "road one, road two, road three," for each leaf he tore off. The final leaf he tore off said road two. Oedipus cheerfully started down road two, not knowing where it would lead.

After a while, Oedipus saw that the road he had chosen led up to a mountain path. He suddenly heard a voice call out to him.

"I would not go that way if I were you!" Oedipus turned to see an old man leaning on a stick.

"Why not?" he asked the man.

"You are heading for Mount Phicium and the Sphinx! Better to go another way," replied the old man, wheezing.

Oedipus realized he was poor and gave him a coin. But he was curious about this creature. He had never heard of anything called a Sphinx.

The old man told him that the Sphinx was sent as punishment to King Laius by the goddess Hera.

"Yes, yes, I have heard of King Laius, but what on earth is a Sphinx?" asked Oedipus.

The old man leaned forward and said, "it is a mortal creature with the head of a woman and the body of a lion. It has wings too, like a bird. It waits for travelers and then asks them riddles. If the traveler fails to reply correctly, it throws them down the mountain to their deaths. So I say, go another way!"

Oedipus was not impressed and said so. He knew that he was good with riddles and went ahead anyway. As he climbed, the pass got narrower and suddenly he was confronted by the Sphinx.

"Halt! You cannot pass," said the creature.

Oedipus saw that the old man's description was spot on. "Why can't I pass?" he asked boldly.

"No one passes without answering my question. If you answer correctly you pass, otherwise..." the Sphinx nodded its head downwards towards the sharp drop of the mountainside.

Oedipus decided to play the game. "What is your question?" he asked.

"What is the thing that walks on four feet in the morning, two feet in the afternoon, and three feet in the evening?" asked the Sphinx, looking keenly at Oedipus.

Oedipus scowled at the Sphinx and replied, "man. When a child, crawls on all fours, when young, he walks on two feet. In the twilight of his age, he walks with the aid of a stick. That would be three feet." The Sphinx was visibly annoyed.

Oedipus then asked a nasty personal question of the Sphinx, who began to flap her wings and dance around in anger. Seeing his chance, Oedipus pushed the Sphinx off the cliff into the valley, killing it.

When he reached the city of Thebes, he was welcomed and honored by the queen and the people. The Sphinx had been a big headache. Ultimately, Oedipus married the queen, whose name was Jocasta, and he lived for a while in Thebes.

## PERSEUS

Perseus was another hero of the Greek myths. His mother was Danae and his father was Zeus.

Acrisius, the father of Danae, was upset that Danae had a child with Zeus. He decided to put Danae and the child in a wooden box and set them adrift in the sea.

The box drifted along for some time until it was picked off the coast of Seriphos by Dictys, who was a fisherman.

Dictys was a kind soul and looked after Danae and her son, who now had a name—Perseus. As the years passed, Perseus grew into a strong and handsome young man. He was, after all, the son of Zeus!

Danae came to know that Dictys was the brother of the king of Seriphos, Polydectes, although he lived in humble surroundings and was an ordinary fisherman.

Polydectes slowly fell in love with Danae and wanted Perseus out of the way so he could come and visit Danae. Polydectes struck upon an idea to get rid of Perseus.

Polydectes sent invitations to all the kings and princes, inviting them to come to a feast and celebrate his intention to seek the hand of Hippodamia, a princess. Perseus too was invited.

There was, however, a catch. The suitor who would win Hippodamia's hand would have to defeat her father in a chariot race. Polydectes planned to use this chariot race as an excuse to get rid of Perseus.

At the feast, Polydectes began to talk to Perseus, who he knew was a little vain and proud.

"I want to win this chariot race, but don't have a good horse," he said casually to Perseus.

Perseus said nothing. He knew that he was poor.

"Well, I was hoping you would help me by giving me your horse," said Polydectes, knowing that Perseus did not have one.

"I don't have a horse, but I will do anything to help you win the race," replied Perseus.

This was what Polydectes was waiting for. "Anything?" he asked Perseus.

Perseus nodded.

Polydectes then sprung his trap. "Well," he said. "I would like you to get me the head of Medusa if you can manage that."

Perseus was headstrong and proud, so he immediately agreed to get Polydectes the head of Medusa, unaware of who Medusa was.

When Danae heard what her son was planning to do, she tried her best to dissuade him. She told him that Medusa was a Gorgon who had snakes for hair, tusks for teeth, and talons for nails. She was a terrifying creature with one deadly weapon—her eyes. Anyone who even glanced at her eyes would turn into stone for all eternity.

Perseus, however, was determined to go. He had given his word in front of a lot of people and he was not about to go back on his promise.

Dictys gave him advice that he should not trust anybody and to be careful. He warned Perseus that the mainland was a difficult place.

Perseus set off and arrived on the mainland. What he saw there baffled him. He saw that people were well-dressed, while he was dressed in very ordinary clothes, which made him stick out as an outsider. He decided that he would need assistance if he was to find Medusa, so he went to the Oracle of Delphi.

The words of the oracle puzzled him. The oracle had said that Perseus must travel to the land where people lived on the fruit of the oak tree. Then an old woman told him what it meant.

She told him that he must go to Dodona, where the trees can speak. There, he would find the answer.

Perseus was crestfallen. This was too much. First the Oracle of Delphi, then speaking trees! But he went to Dodona anyway. As he walked through the oak trees, he heard someone speak. Surprised, he stopped. Could the trees *really* speak?

Suddenly, a young man stepped out from behind the trees. Perseus saw that the man was wearing sandals with wings and carried a staff with two live snakes on it.

"I am Perseus…" began Perseus, but he was stopped by the young man, who said that he knew who Perseus was. This baffled Perseus to no end. How did he know who he was?

Then, something even stranger happened. A beautiful woman stepped out from behind the young man. She was holding a shield.

Perseus was rooted to the spot, his head in a whirl.

The woman, who wore a grave expression, said that they were there to help Perseus on his quest.

"We too, are the children of Zeus, like you," said the woman. Perseus never knew that Zeus was his father, so he was taken aback, but kept quiet.

The woman continued to speak and told Perseus that they would give him the weapons he needed to destroy Medusa.

The young man asked Perseus to take off his shoes. Perseus took them off. To his amazement, he found that the winged shoes of the stranger flew and attached themselves to his feet.

"You can go wherever you wish by just thinking about it," said the young man. "And here is a cape and hood. As long as you wear it, you will remain invisible," he continued, handing the article to Perseus.

The woman, who was silent, now introduced herself as Athena, and the young man as Hermes.

Athena gave the shield to Perseus, telling him to keep it highly polished. She next handed Perseus a short-bladed weapon that looked like a scythe, with the instruction to be careful. The blade was extremely sharp. She also gave him a satchel, which mystified Perseus, but he took it graciously.

Perseus, however, had one question. Where would he find Medusa? Which island did she live on?

Hermes and Athena refused to tell him exactly but told him how to find her.

It seemed that there was a trio of old sisters who lived in a cave in Mysia. They had one eye and one tooth between them and used them in turns, to see and to eat. Perseus used his magic sandals and arrived at the mouth of the cave. Using the cloak and the hood to make himself invisible, he entered the cave. He saw the sisters fighting over who should have the eye and the tooth. He grabbed both. The sisters realized that there was someone in the cave, and grew angry. Perseus asked them where to find Medusa. When the sisters refused to answer, he threatened to throw the eye and tooth into the sea. This worked and he got the answer he wanted—Medusa lived on an island off the coast of Libya.

Leaving the cave, he started flying over the Libyan coast, trying to locate the island. It took him a while to spot it. He saw that all three Gorgon sisters were asleep. Only one had serpents for her hair. *That must be Medusa*, thought Perseus.

Perseus also saw several rock formations, which he realized were men and animals and even some children. They were all victims of Medusa's evil eyes. He knew that, at any cost, he must avoid looking into the eyes of Medusa.

Perseus slowly dropped to within a few feet of the sleeping Medusa. He held the shield and the scythe in front of him, ready to do his job. The snakes in Medusa's head began moving and hissing. As soon as Medusa opened her eyes, she saw her own reflection and let out a shriek. Instantly, Perseus cut off her head and put it in the satchel. He then flew away upwards. He had done what he had come to do.

But his adventures were not over yet.

Flying home, he took a wrong turn and saw a beautiful maiden chained to a rock. He landed beside her and asked her why she was imprisoned. She told Perseus that her name was Andromeda and she had been chained to the rock as a sacrificial offering.

Perseus was intrigued and asked her what she had done to deserve such a fate. She told Perseus that it was the fault of her mother, who had said aloud that she was more beautiful than the spirits of the ocean, the nereids, and others.

Perseus said that he kind of agreed with her mother. Andromeda then told him that Poseidon, angry at this announcement by her mother, had her chained and was going to send a dragon called Cetus to eat her. This was the sacrifice he demanded. Since Poseidon controlled the seas, this had to be done, otherwise, Poseidon threatened to stop all ships coming through.

At this point, Andromeda pointed to the sea and said, "here he comes—Cetus. Now I must die!"

Seeing what appeared to be a monster of some kind approaching, Perseus took out his scythe and dived into the sea.

After a few minutes, he surfaced. There was a lot of blood in the ocean. Andromeda knew that he had slain the monster. Perseus flew to where Andromeda was chained and set her free. "Let's get you home," he said with a smile.

Together they flew to the palace in Ethiopia, where Andromeda was greeted with cries of joy by her mother and father. Shortly thereafter, they were married.

After living in Ethiopia for a while, Andromeda wanted to see Perseus's home. Although Perseus told her that it was a humble cottage, she insisted that she wanted to go and live there. Perseus agreed and together they arrived at Seriphos, the place where Perseus used to live and found the cottage in ruins. It had been burned.

There was no trace of his mother, or of Dictys. Perseus then asked around and was told that Polydectes had arrested them and taken them to his court. Enraged, Perseus picked up his satchel containing the head of Medusa and went to the court of Polydectes. He stood behind the throne on which Polydectes was sitting. He saw his mother and Dictys being brought in, bound with ropes. Perseus waited, and then walked forward.

Polydectes was delighted to see him. "Well, well, if it isn't Perseus!"

Perseus asked Polydectes, "why have you imprisoned my mother and Dictys?"

"Your mother was supposed to marry me. Instead, she married this beggar Dictys!" replied Polydectes in anger. "And now they shall die," he added.

Perseus loudly asked his mother, Dictys, and everyone in the court who was on his side not to look at him, and to keep their eyes on Polydectes.

Perseus then said, "you wanted the head of Medusa, here it is."

He produced the head from the satchel and showed it to Polydectes. The curse of Medusa did its work.

What people saw after that was astonishing and frightening. Polydectes and his guards had all turned into stone statues. That was the end of Polydectes.

It is said that Perseus and Andromeda lived happily for many years.

# CHAPTER 7:
# THE ORACLE OF DELPHI AND OTHER STORIES

## THE ORACLE OF DELPHI

This oracle was very important to the Greeks. Kings, gods, goddesses, and ordinary mortals all came to the oracle to get answers to their problems. The temple of this oracle was in Delphi. How did it come to be in Delphi, and from where did this oracle stuff come from? Thereby hangs a tale.

Do you remember Apollo? The god with the lyre? Well, apart from being a god of many things, he was also an excellent archer, and his arrows never missed their mark.

In this story, we again come across the goddess Hera, the wife of Zeus, who was an exceedingly jealous woman. When she came to know that Zeus had two children from another lady, she was angry. The two children were Apollo and Artemis. They have hidden away on an island. Hera found out and decided to kill them. Sounds pretty cruel, but that's the way it was.

Let's go back a little. Rhea, who was the wife of Cronus, gave her husband a stone to swallow instead of the newborn child Zeus. Cronus had swallowed it thinking it was his sixth child. Zeus, if you remember, gave a potion to Cronus, which made him vomit his siblings, along with the stone that he had swallowed. This stone was thrown away by Zeus and landed at a place called Pytho. The place where it landed became sacred. Gaia, the mother goddess, then brought forth a large serpent to guard the stone and the place where it fell. This serpent was called Python from the place name Pytho. (Snakes still have the name python. These are enormous snakes that can swallow their prey whole!) The serpent was always present and no one dared to go there, as it was too dangerous.

Hera, in her anger, asked the serpent to go and kill Apollo and Artemis. Zeus, who loved his children, sent word to Apollo about what Hera was up to.

Apollo decided to defend himself and his sister. But he needed a powerful weapon. Python was no ordinary serpent. He sent word to Hephaestus, the man who could make magic weapons. Hephaestus toiled away for several days and made a powerful bow and golden arrows. These he gave to Apollo.

Carrying the special weapons, Apollo went to Pytho and lay in wait for the serpent to show itself. When it did appear, Apollo, with unerring aim, shot an arrow through its eye. As the serpent writhed on the ground, dying, Apollo said, "die and rot here forever."

The serpent did rot there, but it was created by the goddess Gaia so its rotting carcass created a chasm. From this chasm rose vapors that, when inhaled, put a person into a trance. Apollo, meanwhile, had renamed Pytho—he called it Delphi.

As word spread about the vapor and its ability to put people into trances, in which state they could foretell the future, it became a popular place. A temple was constructed and a priestess, called Pythia, was appointed. The priestess would go into a trance and reply to the queries that people asked of her.

The problem was that not all the answers from the priestess were clear. Another priest or a wise man was sometimes needed to decode the meaning. (Perseus, if you remember, faced the same problem until an old woman told him what the prophecy meant.) Sometimes the oracle did not reply and this enraged many people. Hercules, being a strong and impatient sort of character, started destroying the temple when he did not get a response. Apollo had to intervene to stop him from doing that.

However, Apollo had another problem. How would he get people to work in the temple? Cleaning and guarding were some of the things that were urgently needed. The place where he had built the temple was deserted. There was no one around who he could engage for this task.

Suddenly, he saw in the distance a ship manned by Cretans. Apollo immediately changed himself into a dolphin and chased the ship. Once he had caught up with it he jumped on board. The Cretans were terrified, especially when they noticed that they had lost control of their vessel and that it was turning around and heading in a different direction. It entered the Sea of Corinth and ran aground on the shores of Crissa. Apollo now changed himself into his divine form and told the sailors not to be afraid.

Apollo then pronounced his will.

"You will never return to your homeland again. You will stay here and guard the temple. Honors and wealth will be yours. Everything that is offered to me, you shall have." said Apollo to the frightened sailors who just nodded in agreement.

"And since you saw me first as a dolphin, you will henceforth address me as 'Delphinian.'"

Apollo had solved his problem. The Cretans did as they were told and the temple had the caretakers it needed.

Over time, the oracle became famous and no god or king ever did anything without a prophecy from the Oracle of Delphi. This oracle has already popped up in several of these stories.

## ZEUS, HADES, AND PERSEPHONE

Zeus, as you already know, was the lord of everything in the universe, above ground. But the lord of the Underground, or Underworld, was Hades and his queen Persephone. Hades and Zeus were also brothers.

Demeter was the goddess who ruled over the growth of everything on Earth. Trees, crops, flowers, all of it. She had a beautiful daughter called Persephone who also caused flowers to bloom and the crops to mature. Flowers would bloom with her mere presence.

One day as Persephone was playing around in a garden, the earth split open and a chariot came charging out of the ground. Before she could do anything, the driver of the chariot, Hades, grabbed her and the chariot disappeared into the crack. Moments later, the crack sealed itself. Persephone had vanished without a trace. As the months passed by, a distraught Demeter was so busy looking for her daughter that she neglected her duties as goddess of the crops and harvest. The Earth began to suffer from famine. Nothing was growing and soon, this news reached Zeus.

Demeter searched everywhere but found no trace of her daughter. Zeus, by this time realizing the danger, got the council together. He was angry that no one had told him about the mysterious disappearance of Persephone.

"And it seems none of you know where she is! What kind of gods are you anyway?" he barked, losing his temper. The gods sat silent.

One day at the council meeting, Helios the sun god suddenly said, "I know what happened to Persephone."

Zeus turned to him. "You know and yet you didn't tell us?"

Helios replied in an offended tone. "Nobody asked me. Everybody thinks I know nothing."

"Well, where is she then?" asked Zeus in anger.

"Hades took her to his palace," said Helios.

Zeus was now really angry. He decided to go to the Underworld and confront Hades immediately.

When he arrived at the Underworld, Zeus went to Hades and demanded an explanation. He also wanted the return of Persephone without any delay.

"On the Earth, there is a famine and people are dying of hunger! What do you think you were doing, kidnapping Persephone?" said Zeus.

Hades refused. "I love her and she will stay with me."

This enraged Zeus even more. He threatened Hades. "You do not know my power yet. I will ask Hermes to bring no more souls to your Underworld. If required, all mortals shall become immortal. You won't have any souls to deal with. You will become the laughing stock of the gods. What are you going to do then?"

Hades knew when he was beaten. But Hades was the lord of the Underworld, and he still had a trick up his sleeve.

"I will return her to you tomorrow. Let her stay for one more day," pleaded Hades.

Zeus agreed and went back happy.

After Zeus had gone, Hades went to the room of Persephone and told her what had happened and that she must go back to her home.

Hades then produced some pomegranate seeds and asked Persephone to eat some. Persephone picked up six seeds and started eating them. Hades watched with gleaming eyes.

The next day Hermes arrived to take Persephone back to the natural world. Hades called Hermes and told him, "you may take her back, but she has eaten the fruit of the Underworld, so she must return here. She has eaten six seeds, so she must come here to me for six months every year. The other six months she can spend on the surface."

Hermes knew that this was true. He agreed and took Persephone and left.

That began the cycle of regeneration of plants and the seasons. When Persephone was on the surface, everything grew and the Earth was fruitful. But when she went back to Hades, trees shed their leaves and winter stopped the growth of crops. Nature held her breath, waiting for the return of Persephone.

## BELLEROPHON AND PEGASUS

Nobody knows for sure who Bellerophon's father was. Some myths say it was Poseidon, but Bellerophon was raised by Glaucus, King of Corinth. His mother was Eurynome.

Bellerophon grew up to be, as with all gods, strong and handsome. He had one special characteristic: He loved horses.

Bellerophon never saw gods performing miracles or hurling thunderbolts in Corinth. It was just a very busy city with lots of normal people.

Then one day he heard something that drew his attention. He was 14 years old and had the curiosity of the young. The rumor was that people had seen a white horse that had wings and could fly. Hearing the rumors, Bellerophon tried to find someone who had actually seen this miraculous creature, but he found no one. He dismissed the rumors as fantasy. But this was to change soon.

Bellerophon heard that certain Corinthians were saying that the flying horse was actually present in an area just outside of Corinth. The horse had been seen drinking from a natural water spring at a place called Pirene. Bellerophon decided to go to Pirene and see for himself.

When he got to Pirene, Bellerophon went to the spring and met some people who were standing around. When he asked them about the horse, they replied that it had flown away as soon as it had heard them approaching. It was an extremely shy animal. Bellerophon decided to hide near the spring and wait. Maybe the horse would come back if of course such a thing really existed.

After a while, Bellerophon fell asleep but was awakened by a soft sound. He carefully raised his head and looked at the spring. He saw the horse—a white horse with wings! Bellerophon looked carefully to see if the wings were attached to the horse with wax or something similar. It was not a prank—the horse had real wings.

Bellerophon tried to quietly creep up to the horse and pet him. But horses have an acute sense, and before Bellerophon could get anywhere near, it galloped, spread its wings, and flew away. Bellerophon stared up in amazement. *I have to have that horse*, he told himself as he returned home.

As the days passed, Bellerophon tried all sorts of tricks to get the horse to come to him, but nothing seemed to work. His mother noticed that something was bothering her son and called in the seer Polyidus.

Polyidus then approached Bellerophon and asked him what the matter was. Bellerophon, after much hesitation, told him. The seer smiled and said that he would tell him how to succeed. Bellerophon was skeptical but listened. He knew that Polyidus had the power of prophecy.

"You must go to the temple of Athena and lie down on the floor and ask for Athena's help. She will definitely help you. There is no other way," said the seer.

Bellerophon was hesitant. He did not believe in gods doing simple favors or working miracles. But Polyidus was a prophet and his words could not be taken lightly.

Bellerophon set out for the temple of Athena. Arriving, he lay down on the floor as directed by Polyidus and waited.

Then he heard a voice. "Bellerophon, you want to ride the white horse? He is shyer than any horse."

Bellerophon nodded his head, not knowing if the gesture was visible to whoever was talking. Then he saw the image of Athena before him and he was amazed. So the gods and goddesses really did exist!

"Only the golden bridle will allow you to ride him. Take it with you," said the goddess before she disappeared.

Bellerophon got up and scratched his head. He did not have a golden bridle. What was the goddess talking about?

Then he saw a bundle on the floor and picked it up. Inside was a golden bridle! *Miracles really did happen*, thought Bellerophon.

Happily, he carried the bridle home, thanked Polyidus for his advice, and prepared to ride Pegasus.

Bellerophon went to the spring where he knew Pegasus came to drink water and waited.

Pegasus arrived as usual and drank from the spring. Bellerophon, golden bridle in hand, approached slowly, making soothing sounds. Pegasus looked nervous but did not run or fly away. Bellerophon put his hand out and patted the horse, and slipped the bridle in place. With a leap, he was astride Pegasus. At his command, the horse slowly started running and, spreading its wings, flew up into the sky.

Bellerophon was ecstatic with joy as he looked down upon Corinth.

After flying around for some time, Bellerophon guided Pegasus to the palace grounds and landed there to everyone's amazement. Many people would come to see this miracle of a flying horse.

## BELLEROPHON AND THE CHIMERA

The king of Lycia, Iobates, wanted Bellerophon dead. The reason is somewhat complicated and is not part of this story. This part is about how Bellerophon killed the dreaded Chimera, a fierce monster that was supposed to be immortal.

Bellerophon knew very well that to get the better of a creature like the Chimera, he needed a special kind of lance. So he went to a good ironsmith and had a lance designed specially for himself.

Sitting astride Pegasus, Bellerophon set off to find the Chimera. As he flew around, he noticed that large tracts of the land were on fire. Wildfires happened often, so Bellerophon paid no attention to them. But the swirling smoke from the fires made it difficult to see the ground below. Then he spotted a deer running for its life and being pursued by what looked like a lion, but was not quite a lion. It had a lion's body and head, but there was a goat's head on top too, complete with horns protruding from the back, and the tail was a snake! It was spouting fire from its mouth. Bellerophon had never seen such a creature. He fired several arrows at it, with no result. Then he guided Pegasus lower and when the creature opened its mouth and started spouting fire, he threw the lance straight into the creature's mouth and down its throat.

The creature began growling and screaming and rolling on the ground. Moments later, it was dead. Bellerophon had very cleverly had the lance made of lead. As soon as the lance entered the lion's body, the lead began to melt from the creature's fiery breath, killing it.

Bellerophon cut off the Chimera's head and took it back to show Iobates, who was definitely not happy to see a half-burned lion's head lying in his throne room.

## ORPHEUS AND EURYDICE

Orpheus is known as the god of good time, fun, and music. His singing was so beautiful that people were hypnotized by it. Orpheus loved his wife Eurydice very much, and when she died of a snake bite and her soul went to the Underworld, he was very sad. He gave up singing and just walked around with an unhappy air around him.

One day Apollo, his father, came to him and asked him how long he would mope around for.

Orpheus did not reply. Apollo asked him again. This time Orpheus said he would be happy if he got his wife, Eurydice, back again. Apollo thought for some time and then said, "in that case, why don't you go and bring her back?"

Orpheus was amazed. "How can I? Nobody who goes to the Underworld ever comes back alive," he said.

"Maybe you can," replied Apollo.

"How?" asked Orpheus, a little surprised.

"Use the power of your music," replied Apollo.

Orpheus sat up. Could that be done?

He decided to try it.

Orpheus took out his lyre, which was lying unused, and restored the instrument.

Then he made a plan. He knew that there were two hurdles to get into the Underworld. The first was Cerberus, the monster who guarded its gates, and the second was the ferryman, Charon, who ran the ferry to the Underworld.

Orpheus started on his journey. When he arrived at the gates, he saw Cerberus ready to pounce on him. He began to play the lyre and sing. Cerberus was hypnotized by the song and slowly fell asleep. Orpheus went past him and arrived at the ferry. There he saw Charon. Before Charon could protest, he began singing. Charon too was charmed and rowed him across to the entrance of the Underworld.

Orpheus, now growing in confidence, entered the Underworld. There, he began serenading the assorted monsters who guarded the place.

Hearing the commotion, Hades and his wife Persephone appeared.

"What are you, a living mortal, doing here?" asked Hades angrily.

"I came to take my wife back to the world of the living," said Orpheus.

"Don't you know that is impossible!" replied Hades.

Persephone, who was listening, spoke to Hades.

Meanwhile, Orpheus could see his wife in the form of a spirit.

Hades then announced that he would permit Orpheus to sing one song, and if he was happy, he would allow him to take his wife back to the world of the living.

Orpheus sang and Hades and Persephone were entranced by the music.

Hades agreed and let her go. Orpheus and his wife Eurydice started walking towards the gates and back to the world of the living.

## ZEUS AND HIS HEADACHE

The great Zeus had a headache. Not an ordinary headache, but a very severe and painful one. He roamed around his palace yelling and screaming, with his hands pressed against the sides of his head. No one knew what to do. Some even thought that war had broken out again.

As Zeus howled in agony, Prometheus arrived at the palace. He took one look at Zeus, turned to Hephaestus, and spoke to him quietly.

Hephaestus hurried away.

What was actually going on in Zeus's head was this:

Metis, who lived inside his head, was forging and making metal objects. These needed hammering. The material for these objects came from the minerals that were present in the food Zeus ate every day. It was no wonder that Zeus felt his head was going to split open.

Prometheus knew about Metis being inside Zeus's head.

After a while, Hephaestus returned from his smithy with a large axe. Prometheus then asked Zeus to kneel down and lower his head in prayer. Zeus knelt and lowered his head. Hephaestus then brought up the axe and with one blow, split open Zeus's head. All the gods and goddesses present were stunned. They were also afraid of what Zeus might now do.

But then something strange began to happen.

From inside the split skull, a figure began to emerge. It was a female figure in full armor. She stepped out of the skull and stood in front of the kneeling Zeus. She addressed him as father.

As if by magic, the split skull closed and became whole again. Zeus stood up and recognized his daughter—Athena.

## HOW THE BEE GOT ITS STING

In the heavens, the marriage of Aphrodite and Hephaestus was announced. Zeus organized a huge banquet and almost all the gods and goddesses were invited. To add a little spice to the proceedings, Zeus said that there would be a competition. The one who prepared the most original and best wedding dish would be rewarded. He would grant them a favor. Everybody brought what they thought were good dishes and a variety of food turned up. Once the wedding celebrations were over, it was time for the selection of the best dish. Zeus went around tasting the dishes. Finally, he arrived at the table of a small creature with wings named Melissa. She had before her a jar of a kind of gooey substance. Zeus dipped his finger and put some in his mouth. It tasted exquisite. Zeus had no hesitation in declaring it the winner. The creature told Zeus that it was honey.

Melissa then flew close to Zeus's ear and said, "my Lord, it is very difficult to make this honey. I have to go from flower to flower for days to produce a small amount. It is very hard work. But the problem is that animals like bears come and take away my honey. I cannot do anything because I am small. I want you to give me something to defend myself against these robbers. The snake that produces nothing has a deadly bite and poison. Give me a weapon that is powerful enough to kill any who come to rob me of my honey."

Zeus was angry that Melissa should ask for such a boon. But he thought awhile and then he said that he would make the collection of honey easier for Melissa. From now on she would have helpers who would collect the honey. She would be the queen. Zeus also granted her a sting, which all bees now have. Melissa was happy that her wish had been granted.

The honeybee is still called *mélissa* in Greek.

## THE LEGEND OF THE MUSES

According to myth, there were nine muses—Clio, Euterpe, Thalia, Melpomene, Terpsichore, Erato, Polyhymnia, Urania, and Calliope.

In the beginning, they were responsible for various things, but ultimately they were said to rule over music and poetry. They served as an inspiration to aspiring artists and poets.

The Muses were the constant companions of Apollo, who was addicted to music, as you already know. They were described as young women with smiling faces, though sometimes grave and thoughtful.

Their offerings were honey, water, and milk.

Nobody knows for sure where the Muses came from, or who were their parents. Some myths say they were the daughters of Uranus and Gaia.

The Muses lived far away from the hustle and bustle of normal life. They preferred the peace and quiet of a mountain called Helicon. The slopes of this mountain were covered with scented plants and flowers, which the Muses loved. They would dance and sing there. The mountain also had several freshwater springs, and anyone who drank its waters would be inspired to write great poetry. At night, the Muses would enclose themselves in clouds and float close to the habitations. The people and gods would hear their beautiful voices singing.

It is said that the Muses were the guardians of the temple of Delphi.

# CHAPTER 8:
# MORE GODS, GODDESSES, AND HEROES

In this chapter, we shall talk about some of the lesser gods, goddesses, and heroes, who, while they were not so well-known as the famous ones, were nevertheless important in their own way. They too played important parts in the lives of the gods and the people.

## THEMIS

Of the lesser gods and goddesses, Themis was important. Themis was the daughter of Uranus and Gaia, the original divinities of the universe. She belonged to the gods called the Titans and despite the defeat of the Titans, was respected and welcomed at the court of the Olympians. She was known to be wise and gave advice to various gods.

When Rhea wanted to hide her sixth child so that Cronus would not swallow it, Themis advised her, took the child from her, and delivered him to the place where he would be safe.

Most of all she is known as the goddess of justice. It was she who had delivered the Oracle of Delphi, which she had inherited from her mother Gaia. She was known as the counselor to everyone and was renowned for her fairness and judgment.

## IRIS

Gaia is said to also be the mother of Iris. Myth says that she was the goddess of the rainbow, and like Hermes, a messenger of the gods. Zeus especially used her to send his messages when Hermes was not available. When Zeus wanted to send a message to the other gods, he would send Iris. When the message was for the mortals on Earth, Iris would descend onto the Earth and assume a mortal form and deliver the message.

She was known to fly using wings attached to her shoulders and sometimes wore winged sandals, like Hermes. Amazingly, she was just as fast through water as she was through the air! She proved her powers when, at the request of Zeus, she dove into the ocean and went to the Underworld to fill a golden cup with water from the river called Styx. As everyone knows, going to the Underworld is not easy, it is way down, deep in the Earth's bowels. This proves just how powerful she was.

## HELIOS

In the Greek myths, Apollo was the god of sunlight, but he was not the sun god. That title belonged to Helios.

The story goes like this: Every morning Helios would emerge from the east from a swamp. He had a golden chariot that had been made by Hephaestus, the great metal worker. Winged horses were fastened to this chariot, white and dazzling in appearance. The horses breathed fire and were indeed extraordinary. This was because Helios was the dazzling sun god, of course!

Astride this chariot, Helios roamed the heavens, casting light on everything. Try to think of it as a sunrise. By midday when Helios had reached the highest point in the heavens, he started moving downwards, and in the evening it looked like he had plunged into the ocean. Actually, he landed inside a golden cup where his family awaited him. He then sailed the cup eastward until he arrived home. He would emerge again the next morning. It is the rising and the setting of the sun each day of our lives. There is another interesting point to note: Helios knew everything that was going on in the universe. No one knew as much as he did.

## EOS

While Helios was the sun god, Eos was the goddess of the dawn—that gentle glow of light that is seen just before the sun rises. Every morning she would rise up in the sky, wearing saffron robes and carrying a torch in her hand. The soft light of dawn was her work. It announced the coming of day and the rising of Helios, the sun god.

## ODYSSEUS

This character in Greek mythology is famous for a story that involves the Sirens. Odysseus was setting out on a voyage when a sorceress called Circe warned him of the Sirens. She told Odysseus never to go to the island where these creatures lived. These dangerous creatures sang so well that most men were unable to keep from going over to the island. Should Odysseus go, he would be tortured by the Sirens and ultimately killed and eaten. Odysseus kept that in mind and this saved his life and that of his crew.

When he was approaching the island where the Sirens lived, Odysseus asked that he be bound to the mast of his vessel. He then put wax into the ears of his crew.

When he came close to the rocky islet where the Sirens lived, he saw them. They were weird creatures—half-woman and half-bird.

Then he heard their song. The sorceress had been right. Odysseus, had he not been bound to the mast, would never have been able to resist the song, and would have gone to the islet. Such was the power of the music that the Sirens produced.

The crew members, of course, could not hear anything, and the ship passed the islet safely.

Later, when the Sirens tried the same trick with the vessel Argo, which was carrying Jason and his army, Orpheus, who was present on the vessel, sang a song of such beauty that the Sirens fell silent. It is said that after this the Sirens lost their ability to sing and were turned into rocks!

## PANDORA

Pandora was not a Greek goddess or anything, but she played an important part in the lives of mortals.

The story begins when Prometheus stole fire from the forge of Hephaestus and gave it to the mortals. Prometheus also taught humans how to use fire.

This made Zeus very, very angry. He loved Prometheus and felt betrayed. The other thing that worried him was the thought that once mortals had the power of fire, they would not need the gods in the future, and would stop making offerings to them. All the good stuff that came from these offerings would disappear! That would not do.

Zeus had Prometheus chained to a rock. This part of the story you already know, but there is another part that needs to be told now.

Prometheus had a brother called Epimetheus. Epimetheus was not as clever as Prometheus.

Zeus, before he had Prometheus chained to the rock, summoned Hephaestus, the god who could work miracles with his hands.

"Fashion a beautiful woman for me out of clay," he commanded Hephaestus.

"Yes, my Lord," replied Hephaestus, wondering what Zeus had in mind.

Hephaestus went back to his workshop and fashioned a clay figure of a woman of exquisite beauty. Aphrodite breathed life into her. All the other gods and goddesses pitched in and gave her jewelry and other ornaments.

Zeus then called to her, "I will give you a vase with a sealed top. You must take this with you to the land of the mortals. But you must never open it!"

Zeus named the beautiful woman Pandora and sent her down to Epimetheus.

Prometheus knew that his brother was not very intelligent and always did things without thinking. Before leaving for distant lands to teach mortals the use of fire, he had warned Epimetheus not to accept any gifts that Zeus might send. Prometheus knew that Zeus was going to try and punish him for stealing fire. He was afraid that Zeus would target Epimetheus, and he was right.

Pandora appeared before Epimetheus, brought to him by Hermes. Epimetheus fell in love with her immediately.

Epimetheus married her and they began living together. Pandora kept the vase without opening it, but she often wondered what was in it.

One day she could not resist her curiosity and went and opened the lid of the vase. Out flew disease, anger, and all of the nasty things that mortals are suffering from even today.

Seeing that ugly things were coming out, she quickly put the lid back on, but it was too late. All the nasties had escaped and they began to spread all over the world.

Zeus had known all along that Pandora would open the lid of the vase.

Pandora was very sad and Epimetheus understood too late why Zeus had sent Pandora to him. He wondered what Prometheus would say when he came back.

## CADMUS AND THE CITY OF THEBES

In Greek mythology, the city of Thebes was very important. But how it was founded is part of an interesting story.

Cadmus (who is the hero of this story) was from a place called Tyre. As it happened, his sister Europa had gone missing. Cadmus's parents sent him to find and bring back his sister. Cadmus took with him a clever and beautiful lady called Harmonia, who he met in a place called Samothrace. He also took with him a gang of men as part of his entourage.

As they wandered around looking for Europa, Cadmus decided that he would need help, so they headed for the Oracle of Delphi. Cadmus, however, was already famous for creating the alphabet. People could now communicate, and everyone sang his praise. He was also known for his athletic prowess.

When they reached the temple at Delphi, Cadmus entered and then asked the question to which he was seeking the answer.

“How do I find my sister?” Cadmus asked the oracle. As usual, the reply was vague.

The oracle said that Cadmus must follow a cow with a crescent moon mark on her back until it lay down with exhaustion. At the spot where the cow lay down, Cadmus must build.

That was all. Cadmus was totally baffled by the prophecy. He could make no head or tail of it. What cow? Build what? He was looking for his sister, that was all. Annoyed, he walked away from the oracle. Even Harmonia was unable to decode this strange message. They continued on their way, still not sure where to look for Europa. The oracle had been of no help at all.

The temple of Delphi was situated in an area called Phocis. The king of Phocis, Pelagon, when he heard that the famous Cadmus was in his area, sent out an invitation for him to come and rest awhile in the royal palace. The tired Cadmus, Harmonia, and his band of men accepted gratefully.

After a meal, Cadmus and Harmonia were strolling in the palace grounds together when the father of Pelagon approached them suddenly. He was a little drunk. He told them that he wanted Cadmus to take part in a local sports event that was slated to start the next day. The king too, as it turned out, wanted Cadmus to participate.

It was just a local event and Cadmus won most of the events easily. The king, who was not very rich, did not know what to give as a special present. A while later, one of the king's henchmen arrived with a cow in tow. The king asked Cadmus to accept the cow as a gift. The courtiers and the public laughed at such a silly prize. But it was Harmonia who suddenly saw the significance of the cow.

"Look Cadmus, the cow!" she said, pointing excitedly at the animal.

"Yes, I see it. It's a cow. So what?" replied Cadmus, somewhat annoyed.

Harmonia still tugged at Cadmus's hand. "Yes, but look at the mark on its back!"

It was then that Cadmus saw the mark of the crescent moon on the back of the cow.

"Whoa!" exclaimed Cadmus, realizing that this was the animal that the oracle had spoken about.

The cow, meanwhile, had started wandering off. Cadmus quickly thanked the king for his superb gift, and together with Harmonia, started after the animal. His entourage of men followed.

Cadmus and Harmonia followed the animal over land and vale. Cadmus by now was getting a little fed up with it all. Where was the cow heading, and why did it not stop and rest?

After a while, the cow suddenly sank down onto the ground, unable to carry on. Harmonia was excited. "Just as the oracle said! You must build here."

Cadmus looked at her and asked sarcastically, "build what?"

Harmonia thought for a while and then said, "let us sacrifice the cow to Athena and see what happens." Immediately, a camp was set up.

Cadmus asked his men to fetch water from a nearby spring and he sacrificed the cow to the goddess. As soon as he had done that, some of his men came running back and said that a giant serpent guarding the spring had killed two of his men.

Cadmus wearily got up and went to see what the serpent was all about. He picked up a large boulder and waited. When the serpent appeared, he threw the boulder at it and crushed its skull, killing it. As soon he did that he heard an unseen voice curse him for killing the serpent. Cadmus ignored the curse and came back to camp.

The goddess Athena appeared in front of them and said that she was pleased with the sacrifice. She then advised Cadmus that he must follow her instructions exactly, so that he may overcome the curse placed on him for killing the serpent.

Cadmus agreed to do her bidding.

Athena then told Cadmus to make a plow and make furrows in the land using the plow. Once done, he had to extract the teeth of the serpent and plant each tooth in the furrows. Cadmus fashioned a plow and made the furrows, with his men pulling the plow. He then extracted around 500 teeth from the serpent and planted them in the furrows.

Armed men began to grow out of the earth! One for each tooth buried. Cadmus was puzzled.

The men then formed a group and began advancing onwards Cadmus and his men. Cadmus picked a large stone and hurled it at the advancing men. It hit one of them, and they started fighting amongst themselves. After a while, just five of them remained. Cadmus managed to persuade them into surrendering.

He then asked the men if they knew the name of the place where they were standing.

One of the warriors did know. "It is the plain of Thebes."

Cadmus then announced that he would build a great city right there.

Harmonia, standing and watching this whole scene, smiled to herself. The oracle had been dead right, down to the last detail.

This was how the great ancient city of Thebes was built. The myth, however, does not tell us if Cadmus found his sister.

## PHRYGIA AND THE GORDIAN KNOT

This story is not about a god. It is about an ordinary mortal who became king. How he became king is fascinating to read.

A poor and ambitious peasant named Gordias lived in a place called Macedonia. He used to work the barren fields and live simply. He did not have much money.

One day an eagle flew down and perched on the pole of his oxcart. The eagle looked at him with stern eyes and did not move. Gordias, initially puzzled, took it as a sign that the gods were smiling at him. He thought that he was destined for greater things.

He removed the plow from his cart and decided to go to the oracle of Zeus. The funny thing was that the eagle refused to move even as Gordias drove the cart over rocky paths.

On the way, he met a beautiful girl who he found had prophetic powers. He wanted to take her with him. The first thing this girl said to Gordias was to hurry up and get to the oracle. Gordias agreed to take her with him, only if she agreed to marry him. She nodded her head and said yes.

As this was going on, it so happened that the king of Phrygia suddenly died and left no heirs. The people were worried. Who would now be king? They hurried to the oracle of Zeus to get an answer. The oracle told them that they should crown the first person to enter their gates in a cart. The people were happy and went to their city and waited at the gates to see who would come in a cart.

Meanwhile, Gordias arrived at the gates of Phrygia. The people saw that he was driving a cart and immediately asked him to be king. The eagle had flown away the moment Gordias entered the gates.

Once he was crowned king, Gordias began to rule, and he ruled really well. The oxcart in which he had arrived was treated as a holy relic by the people. They set up a wooden post and tied the yoke of the cart to it using a very complicated knot. The knot was created by Gordias and was so complex that nobody could untangle it. Many warriors and brave men tried but failed. The knot remained secure. It became known as the Gordian Knot. Even today, when a problem is very complicated and difficult to solve, it is referred to as a Gordian Knot!

There is also an interesting ending to this story.

This knot lay unopened for about a thousand years, till a great Macedonian warrior called Alexander came to Phrygia. When he learned about this knot, he went to take a look at it. After looking at it, he drew his sword, and with one slice he cut the knot. He later became famous for his many conquests, and is known as Alexander the Great!

Gordias now takes us to the next story, that of King Midas, who was his son.

## MIDAS

Gordias died after a few years and Midas became king. He was a kind and gentle ruler. But he had one passion—roses. He created a magnificent rose garden and spent most of his time there smelling his lovely roses. He was always respectful, especially to elders.

One day he was walking around his rose garden when he tripped over an old and ugly man who was sleeping. He apologized and invited the man to his palace to eat. The old man agreed. What Midas did not know was that the old man was Silenus, a close companion of the god Dionysus.

Silenus stayed at the palace for 10 days and almost emptied all of Midas's wine and food. Then on the 11th day he said he wanted to leave. Midas was glad. This man had finished a huge amount of his wine and food. Midas was not a rich king, although he wished he had more money to spend on improving his people's lives.

Silenus then asked Midas to escort him to his home. Midas agreed, and along with some of his palace guards, went with Silenus.

After a few days of traveling, they came upon the camp of the god Dionysus. Midas, to his amazement, saw that everyone was drinking and having a merry time.

Silenus introduced Midas to Dionysus, saying that Midas was an extremely good host and that he, Silenus, had drunk all of his wine.

Dionysus looked at Midas and said, "you seem like a kind-hearted soul. Thank you for your hospitality towards my friend Silenus."

Midas just mumbled and nodded his head. He wanted to get back to the palace and his roses. But Dionysus was not finished yet.

"Ask for whatever you want, and I shall grant your wish!" said Dionysus.

"Anything I wish for?" asked Midas. His mind began to race.

"Anything!" replied Dionysus.

Midas was not sure if Dionysus was joking or not. He did appear a little drunk.

Midas thought hard. He decided that if he had a little more money, he could spend it on important things for his kingdom. He would ask for wealth!

"Whatever I touch will turn into gold. That is my wish!" he said.

Dionysus smiled. "Are you sure that is your wish?"

Midas nodded his head vigorously. "Yes, my Lord, that is my wish."

"Granted. Go back home, and use wine to take a bath. Then go to sleep. The next morning, your wish will come true," said Dionysus.

Midas went home happy. He was still a little skeptical but decided to do what he was told to do.

The next morning Midas awoke as usual and went to the rose garden to touch and smell his lovely roses—and got the shock of his life.

As soon as he touched the rose plant and the roses, they turned into gold! Midas could not believe his eyes. He went around touching other rose plants, with the same result. He was overjoyed. Now he had more wealth than anyone in the world, and he could keep creating more and more gold. He started shouting in joy. His wife, hearing his cries, ran out of the palace and came to see what was going on. She had their infant daughter in her arms. Midas, overjoyed, put his arms around her. Bam! His wife and daughter were now golden statues! Midas was taken aback. What had he done? But this was not the end. Whatever food he touched also turned into gold. Within days, Midas was hungry and extremely unhappy. He did not know what to do, or how to get rid of the wish. Then one night, Dionysus appeared in his dream.

"Foolish man! Always be careful what you wish for! Go to the river Pactolus and dip your hand into its waters. The golden touch will be washed away. Dip everything you turned into gold in the same river, and they will all become normal again," said Dionysus, and the dream ended.

The next morning Midas went to the river and did as directed by Dionysus. His golden touch was no more. He took everything that he had touched to the river, including his wife and child, and dipped them. They all returned to their original form. Midas heaved a sigh of relief! He realized that he had been very foolish.

However, the story of Midas has another twist.

After his episode with the golden hands, Midas lost all love for money and wealth. He became the follower of the god Pan, who was always playing on his flute and enjoying life. Midas liked Pan.

One day when Pan was playing the flute, the god Apollo appeared. All present became silent. Apollo played on his lyre and divine music filled the air. Everyone clapped and said that Apollo was the best musician. But Midas disagreed and said so.

"Pan is a better musician," he said. Apollo could not believe his ears and asked Midas to repeat his statement, which he did.

"You have the ears of a donkey," said Apollo.

Within seconds, a new pair of ears began to grow on Midas's head. They were the ears of a donkey. Everyone saw the ears and started to laugh.

Midas ran away, embarrassed. He put on a turban to hide the ears, and went back home.

Midas was aware of his problem and kept wearing the turban so that nobody would know about the ears. But there was one person who had to know, and that was his barber. Midas swore him to silence and threatened to destroy him and his family if he ever let the secret out. The barber was silent for a long time, but he was dying to tell someone. One day, unable to bear the burden of the secret any longer, he went and dug a hole in the ground. Placing his mouth close to the hole he shouted, "the king has the ears of a donkey!" As soon as he said that, he covered the hole with earth so that the secret would not escape. But a seed had fallen into the hole. From the seed grew a sapling, which pierced the earth and came out of the ground. It began whispering in the wind, "the king has the ears of a donkey." Soon, other trees picked up the whisper and the secret finally reached the city. People started laughing and making fun of Midas.

There are two lessons in this story. The first is to be careful of what you wish for, and second is to be careful of what you say.

## THE GREAT FLOOD

Everyone knows about the Great Flood and Noah's Ark. A lot of cultures have a similar story, and there is one in Greek mythology too.

First, a little background. Prometheus married and had a son called Deucalion. Prometheus knew that Zeus was looking for an excuse to destroy all the humans on Earth. Zeus still hated mortals, who were now multiplying and becoming larger in number by the day. Prometheus taught his son everything that would be needed for survival should Zeus do something. That included the craft of carpentry. Together, they built a large wooden box and stocked it with supplies.

Meanwhile, Pandora and Epimetheus too had a daughter, Pyrrha. Deucalion and Pyrrha fell in love and married.

One day, a king called Lycaon, angered Zeus, and Zeus turned him into a wolf. Lycaon's son Nyctimus tried to rule, but his 49 other brothers were destroying everything and setting the land of the mortals on fire. There was mayhem on Earth.

Zeus wanted an excuse, and now he had one. He created huge clouds and they brought down a storm on Earth that drowned every human being. Mankind ceased to exist, except for Deucalion and Pyrrha. They had placed themselves on the wooden box that Deucalion had made, on his father Prometheus's advice. They floated around until the waters subsided. They found that they were on Mount Parnassus. But the slime and mud were thick on the ground. They had to wait for a few more days for it to dry up.

They realized, however, that they were old and could not help bring children to repopulate the Earth. They decided to go to the Oracle of Delphi.

The oracle, as usual, said something not easily understood. It said that they should cover their heads and throw the bones of their mothers over their shoulders.

Deucalion and Pyrrha thought that since their mothers were probably drowned in the flood, how could they find their bones?

But it was Pyrrha who solved the mystery. She picked up a stone and threw it idly. The stone rolled away and suddenly, Pyrrha understood what the oracle was saying. She turned to Deucalion and said, "stones and rocks, that's what we must use. The Earth Mother is Gaia. She is also our mother. We all came from her!"

Deucalion knew that Pyrrha was right. They covered their heads and started throwing stones over their shoulders in every direction. Wherever the stones and rocks landed, young boys and girls began to appear. The Earth began to be populated with people once again.

It is said that we are all descendants of these boys and girls.

# CONCLUSION

By now, you have read most of the interesting mythological stories that the Greeks had created. Some stories have different beginnings and some have different endings. This is because not much is certain about who wrote what. Different writers of ancient Greece have written their own ideas of the myths, but most of the important stories that are here are more or less the best versions.

You should know that Hercules, who is well-known as the mythical strong man, is also called Heracles, but 'Hercules' is what is most popular.

It is not possible to write all the mythological stories in detail, since Greek mythology is huge, with many gods, goddesses, heroes, and mortals all involved in various deeds and conspiracies. There are wars, battles, revenge killings, and other stuff, as you have already read about.

From the story of Hercules, you must have learned about courage and the ability to get the job done, no matter how difficult.

The stories of Perseus and Theseus are very intriguing and exciting. They go through so many problems and pitfalls, but by their courage and cleverness, manage to come out victorious.

Similarly, the story of Icarus and Daedalus teaches us to listen to good advice, especially when it is given by elders. Daedalus, if you remember, warned Icarus not to fly too close to the sun. But Icarus ignored the warning, his wings fell off and he was killed.

The story of Prometheus is very endearing. He knew that he would be punished by Zeus when he stole fire and gave it to the mortals. But he sacrificed his own interest to do so. The punishment that he received was cruel and barbaric, but his action was selfless. He did it for us, mankind.

Greek myth, like all myths, has a number of heroic characters. If you look at history, you will see that heroes are always needed to show the way, and encourage us.

Greek myths are vast, and there are many stories and adventures. They will tell you about exciting places and about how gods and goddesses behaved, sometimes exactly like humans. And it is possible that you may do something heroic someday too—something worth writing a story about.

# REFERENCES

**GREEK MYTHOLOGY FOR KIDS: EXPLORE TIMELESS TALES & BEDTIME STORIES FROM ANCIENT GREECE. MYTHS, HISTORY, FANTASY & ADVENTURES OF THE GODS, GODDESSES, TITANS, HEROES, MONSTERS & MORE**


Adkins, A. W. H., & Richard, J. (2018). Greek mythology | gods, stories, & history. In *Encyclopædia Britannica.* https://www.britannica.com/topic/Greek-mythology

Cavendish, R. (1974). *Man, myth, & magic: An illustrated encyclopedia of the supernatural.* Marshall Cavendish.

Fry, S. (2019). *Mythos: The greek myths reimagined.* Chronicle Books.

Fry, S. (2020). *Heroes: The greek myths reimagined.* Chronicle Books.

Graves, R., & Guirand, F. (1968). *New Larousse encyclopedia of mythology.* Hamlyn.

*Greek mythology.* (2010). Greekmythology.com. https://www.greekmythology.com/

# OTHER BOOKS BY HISTORY BROUGHT ALIVE

- Ancient Egypt: Discover Fascinating History, Mythology, Gods, Goddesses, Pharaohs, Pyramids, and More from the Mysterious Ancient Egyptian Civilization.

Available now on Kindle, Paperback, Hardcover & Audio in all regions

- Greek Mythology: Explore The Timeless Tales Of Ancient Greece, The Myths, History & Legends of The Gods, Goddesses, Titans, Heroes, Monsters & More

Available now on Kindle, Paperback, Hardcover & Audio in all regions

- Mythology for Kids: Explore Timeless Tales, Characters, History, & Legendary Stories from Around the World. Norse, Celtic, Roman, Greek, Egypt & Many More

Available now on Kindle, Paperback, Hardcover & Audio in all regions

- Mythology of Mesopotamia: Fascinating Insights, Myths, Stories & History From The World's Most Ancient Civilization. Sumerian, Akkadian, Babylonian, Persian, Assyrian and More

Available now on Kindle, Paperback, Hardcover & Audio in all regions

- Norse Magic & Runes: A Guide To The Magic, Rituals, Spells & Meanings of Norse Magick, Mythology & Reading The Elder Futhark Runes

Available now on Kindle, Paperback, Hardcover & Audio in all regions

- Norse Mythology, Vikings, Magic & Runes: Stories, Legends & Timeless Tales From Norse & Viking Folklore + A Guide To

The Rituals, Spells & Meanings of Norse Magick & The Elder Futhark Runes. (3 books in 1)

Available now on Kindle, Paperback, Hardcover & Audio in all regions

- Norse Mythology: Captivating Stories & Timeless Tales Of Norse Folklore. The Myths, Sagas & Legends of The Gods, Immortals, Magical Creatures, Vikings & More

Available now on Kindle, Paperback, Hardcover & Audio in all regions

- Norse Mythology for Kids: Legendary Stories, Quests & Timeless Tales from Norse Folklore. The Myths, Sagas & Epics of the Gods, Immortals, Magic Creatures, Vikings & More

Available now on Kindle, Paperback, Hardcover & Audio in all regions

- Roman Empire: Rise & The Fall. Explore The History, Mythology, Legends, Epic Battles & Lives Of The Emperors, Legions, Heroes, Gladiators & More

Available now on Kindle, Paperback, Hardcover & Audio in all regions

- The Vikings: Who Were The Vikings? Enter The Viking Age & Discover The Facts, Sagas, Norse Mythology, Legends, Battles & More

Available now on Kindle, Paperback, Hardcover & Audio in all regions

Made in the USA
Las Vegas, NV
16 October 2024

96928696R00066